The *a la muerte* soldier took another step closer accompanied by the clink of metal on metal

The Executioner sprang from his hiding spot, driving his left hand forward to grasp the guy's throat, striking hard at the exposed torso with his right. The Tanto's cold blade sliced through clothing and sank in up to the hilt. Bolan felt the man shudder as he slid the knife left to right to extend the wound.

Bolan pulled the weakening man in against the log, leaning on him hard. When all movement ceased, he pulled out the knife and cleaned the steel blade against the man's shirt, then sheathed it.

He could hear faint noises coming from the headset the man was wearing. Bolan slipped it off the body, held the earpiece close and listened to the transmission.

"Enrico, what is going on? Talk to me. Where are you?"

"I found him," Bolan said, keeping his voice low. "You want to come and see?"

There was a brief silence.

"Who are you?"

"The one you cannot find. The one who is going to send you to hell."

MACK BOLAN ®
The Executioner

THE EXECUTIONER

DON PENDLETON'S

THE CARTEL HIT

A GOLD EAGLE BOOK FROM

WORLDWIDE®

TORONTO • NEW YORK • LONDON
AMSTERDAM • PARIS • SYDNEY • HAMBURG
STOCKHOLM • ATHENS • TOKYO • MILAN
MADRID • WARSAW • BUDAPEST • AUCKLAND

Recycling programs
for this product may
not exist in your area.

First edition May 2015

ISBN-13: 978-0-373-64438-4

Special thanks and acknowledgment to
Mike Linaker for his contribution to this work.

The Cartel Hit

There is no witness so terrible and no accuser so powerful as the conscience that dwells within us.
—Sophocles

Some men don't have a conscience, or choose to ignore it. When conscience fails, that's where I step in. With guns blazing.
—Mack Bolan

THE
MACK BOLAN
LEGEND

Nothing less than a war could have fashioned the destiny of the man called Mack Bolan. Bolan earned the Executioner title in the jungle hell of Vietnam.

But this soldier also wore another name—Sergeant Mercy. He was so tagged because of the compassion he showed to wounded comrades-in-arms and Vietnamese civilians.

Mack Bolan's second tour of duty ended prematurely when he was given emergency leave to return home and bury his family, victims of the Mob. Then he declared a one-man war against the Mafia.

He confronted the Families head-on from coast to coast, and soon a hope of victory began to appear. But Bolan had broken society's every rule. That same society started gunning for this elusive warrior—to no avail.

So Bolan was offered amnesty to work within the system against terrorism. This time, as an employee of Uncle Sam, Bolan became Colonel John Phoenix. With a command center at Stony Man Farm in Virginia, he and his new allies—Able Team and Phoenix Force—waged relentless war on a new adversary: the KGB.

But when his one true love, April Rose, died at the hands of the Soviet terror machine, Bolan severed all ties with Establishment authority.

Now, after a lengthy lone-wolf struggle and much soul-searching, the Executioner has agreed to enter an "arm's-length" alliance with his government once more, reserving the right to pursue personal missions in his Everlasting War.

Prologue

His name was Hermano Escobedo. Mexican by birth. He came from a small village in Chihuahua, where there was little opportunity to further himself. Four years previously he had traveled across the border into Texas, encouraged by a longtime friend who had done the same thing a couple years earlier and found work. When his friend had the means to send money to Escobedo, he'd told him to make the journey. America was where Escobedo could earn a living. He could send cash to his remaining family—his aging grandfather and grandmother. The offer was too good to pass up, and Escobedo finally made the trip.

Initially, things worked out well. Escobedo's friend helped him get established, pointed him in the right direction to find work. He learned to speak the language. He was smart and had a good ear. It helped. In the Texas town of Broken Tree, the young Mexican showed a willingness to take on a number of jobs.

Escobedo's background was farming. He had a flair for gardening and built a small but steady number of clients. His touch with flowers and plants gained him more customers. He was able to save a little money and his long-term plan was to provide for his grandparents. He found himself a small apartment in Broken Tree. It was nothing grand, but to Hermano Escobedo it was a step up from the tiny place he had shared with his grandparents. Then, two years into his time in America, he received the news that his grandparents had passed away. The priest in the village handled the funerals, so Escobedo had little incentive to return to Mexico.

When he received an offer to tend the gardens at the out-of-town estate belonging to a man named Seb Jessup, Escobedo accepted. One of his Broken Tree clients had referred him to Jessup. When Escobedo first saw the place, he was overwhelmed. It was huge, a great, sprawling house surrounded by lawns and gardens. There were stables for the many horses the man owned. Barns to house machinery. It was always busy, with people coming and going all the time. Expensive cars. Smiling young women. It could have been all too much for a simple *peon* from Chihuahua, but Escobedo had a steady head on his shoulders. He pushed the glamorous lifestyle out of his mind and simply took on the work offered.

Everything went well at first. Jessup sent a car for him three days a week, though Escobedo rarely saw his employer. In fact, he had only ever seen the man once to speak to. That had been on the day he accepted the job. The drive from town took just under twenty minutes, and the day began early and ended late. Escobedo was given charge of the operation. There was a fully equipped workshop that contained all the tools he would ever need, and while the workload was heavy, he took it in stride.

After a few weeks, Escobedo became accepted among Jessup's other employees, to the point that hardly anyone paid him much attention. And Escobedo simply blended in. He was paid at the end of each week by a man named Hatton, who seemed to be Jessup's right-hand man. Hatton said little.

Escobedo's friend, being ambitious, had moved on. He had packed his belongings into his car and driven out of Broken Tree, leaving Escobedo to his new life. It didn't worry him too much. He had always been a solitary person. It was only in the evenings that he felt out of place, but long days of physical labor left him exhausted, and he retired early most nights, knowing his day would start early. When he was not working at the Jessup place, he had his local customers to tend to.

It did not concern Escobedo that there were times when the atmosphere of the Jessup estate changed. Became tense. Agitation seeping in through the calm. Escobedo had learned early on to stick to his own affairs, not to involve himself in matters beyond his purview. He had heard rumors about Seb Jessup, that some of his enterprises were on the risky side. Perhaps even unlawful. Escobedo closed his mind to these rumors. He had steady work. No one bothered him and whatever his employer got up to was none of his business.

That was because he had no idea what was really going on around him. He stayed below the radar. His friend, shortly after Escobedo had arrived in Texas, had explained the facts of life:

"Remember who you are. Do your work. Be humble and do not ask questions. Leave your curiosity at home each day. Be what you are. Invisible. The laborer. Have no shadow. Understand this and you will survive. Make noise and you will pay the price."

Even though he kept a low profile, Escobedo could not escape hearing the gossip of the other Hispanic employees. Some worked inside the house, others in the body shop where Jessup's extensive fleet of cars and SUVs were parked. Escobedo picked up murmurs. Tried to remain indifferent, but words stuck. Remained in his memory.

Words like *illegals*.

Wetbacks.

Transients from across the border.

Once heard, these words became a permanent fixture in Escobedo's thoughts. He wanted to ask questions, but his friend's advice made him hold his tongue. So he watched and listened. There was inside him a sense of morality that refused to allow him to ignore those words. And the harder he tried to dispel them, the stronger the need to know more plagued him.

The urge to understand grew, and he watched and listened more intently.

His friend's advice teased him. *Leave your curiosity at home each day.* But Escobedo's need to know would not let him rest.

He understood the regime that exploited Mexican labor. The shadowy businesses that brought in cheap workers, in the same position as he was. People who wanted to work. To enjoy a better quality of life. They all knew it was a risk, that they would be paid only the minimum, yet they still came, because even that was better for many of them than the life they had in Mexico.

Escobedo had been luckier. His friend had obtained a work permit for him, the piece of paper that made him official. Having someone vouch for him had made life easier. At least Escobedo did not have to survive like a criminal. He could walk the streets with impunity. He wished things were better, but at least here in America he felt safer than in Mexico. And if he worked hard he would eventually become an American citizen.

Then the day came when a situation developed and drew Escobedo to it with its addictive power.

He had been on his knees behind the thick shrubs he was pruning, so was unseen by the men who made their way through the gardens and vanished inside one of the large barns. Something in the way they moved caught Escobedo's interest, and he heard one of them speak as he passed within ten feet of him, seemingly unaware of the Mexican's presence.

"Damn illegals. Jessup will make them pay this time…"

Escobedo had waited until the men were all inside the barn, then took a roundabout route that brought him to the far side of the building. As he slid against the wall, he heard a voice that was unmistakably Jessup's. The man was angry, almost ranting. Escobedo eased his way to a side door and slipped through it. The sound of Jessup's voice filled the interior of the barn. Escobedo snaked his way through the collection of farm implements until he was able to see what was happening.

And wished he hadn't.

He knew right then that his earlier indifference to the rumors floating around had allowed these things to continue. He had learned things about Jessup that he should have reported, yet his concern for his own safety had forced him to stand back, trying to convince himself he should stay clear.

Leave your curiosity at home.

A half dozen of Jessup's men were gathered in a loose crowd around a pair of kneeling Mexicans. The man and woman were young, already bleeding from blows to their faces. Their hands were tied behind their backs. Seb Jessup stood over them, his angry words echoing off the rafters.

Escobedo caught fragments of his tirade, which had to do with lost money, betrayal, risking Jessup's business and threatening his livelihood...

Without thinking, Escobedo pulled his cell phone from his pocket. He trained the camera on Jessup and the kneeling Mexicans. He had no idea how he could help the young couple, but he felt compelled to do something. Anything. Because the terrible feeling sweeping over him told him something bad was about to happen.

One of the men stepped forward and handed something to Jessup.

It was a wooden baseball bat, and without pausing, Jessup swung it, striking first the girl, then the young man.

The sickening sound would stay with Escobedo for a long time. The crunch of the hard wood against weaker skulls. Jessup alternated between his two victims, and their pained cries filled Escobedo's ears. Terrible sounds. Even when the pair slumped forward, Jessup kept up the barrage. Blood flew in bright sprays. The young couple flopped on the barn floor, bodies jerking and twitching as the estate owner battered them in a frenzy of rage. Jessup was spattered with red, yet he still kept up the attack, until one of his men told him the man and woman were dead. He stepped back, panting from his exertions as he stared at the splintered bone and brain matter oozing from the misshapen skulls.

Jessup threw down the bloodied baseball bat.

"Get rid of them," he said. "And when you meet with those Mexican traffickers, tell 'em what happened. Put the fear of God into those fuckers…"

Escobedo felt a presence. He turned and looked into the face of one of Jessup's men.

"Hey, you greaser son of a bitch." The man reached out to grab hold of him.

Escobedo swung around and instinctively lashed out with his free hand, more in panic than resistance. His bunched fist slammed against the other man's jaw. The sound of the blow was loud. The guy spun away from Escobedo, dazed by the strike. His legs gave and he fell to his knees.

Escobedo didn't stay around to see what else was happening. He understood his position. He had witnessed Seb Jessup commit two brutal murders. There was no way the man could allow that to go unpunished.

Escobedo remembered the baseball bat, dripping

with the blood of the two victims. That could be his fate if he didn't move.

He pushed the cell phone into his pocket, then turned and ran across the barn to the door where he'd entered. He shouldered it open and went through. Legs pumping, driven by pure fear, he ran through the gardens and around to the front of the big house. As he crossed the paved drive, he was confronted by the ever-present collection of vehicles parked there.

His thoughts of escape pressured him to go to the closest vehicle, a heavy Ford 4x4. As he yanked open the driver's door, he saw the keys hanging from the ignition. Escobedo climbed in, fumbled with the key, then felt the powerful engine burst into life. He dropped the handbrake, yanked the lever into Drive and stepped on the gas pedal. The 4x4 lurched forward, tires burning against the asphalt. Escobedo fought the wheel as the vehicle turned. He felt it slam against the side of one of the other parked cars, then he got control and headed toward the exit.

He had no fixed destination in mind. His only thoughts were to get away from Jessup and his crew. Escobedo knew they would be coming after him. He was not an experienced driver and thanked God that the roads in Texas tended to run straight. The Ford hurtled onward, responding to his foot on the pedal, and the engine roared as the vehicle gathered speed.

Tangled questions fought for space in his mind.

What to do?

Where to go?

Who could he trust?

He glanced in the rearview mirror.

Several vehicles were on his tail. They were still a distance away, but Escobedo knew that would change.

He had made a bad mistake. One that could end with him sprawled out on that barn floor, his body beaten and bloody. Jessup standing over him, rage in his eyes as he battered him to death. Escobedo had gone into the barn without a clear thought in his head, intent on finding out what was happening, not considering the implications.

He had confirmed his suspicions, but had he expected to simply walk out and inform the authorities? Now none of that mattered.

Hermano Escobedo had exposed himself, and his discovery has plunged him into this nightmare.

Stories about traffickers should have warned him. They bought and sold human lives, their only concern the money they made from the business. One more dead Mexican would pass unnoticed.

Unless he could escape from them.

Escobedo stared through the windshield. How would he get away? They were already following him, and he knew they would not give up. He had witnessed the cruel deaths of the two young Mexicans. Jessup needed to make sure the knowledge went no further.

Broken Tree lay before Escobedo. He realized he might not find any kind of salvation in the town. Seb Jessup was well-known here, while he himself was practically a stranger. He couldn't think of one person he could go to, and a wave of despair washed over him. Violence and death such as this had never featured in his life. It made him think that leaving Mexico had been a mistake. Life in his home village might have been slow and lacking in opportunity, yet there had been no reason to imagine anything like his present situation. Right now, he would welcome his pedestrian existence in Ascensión.

Despite his fear, Escobedo remembered what he had seen. Two young lives wiped out in an instant. Hopes and dreams gone. All because of Jessup's rage and animal brutality. His own safety suddenly didn't seem so important.

He failed to see the bend in the otherwise straight road until he reached it. Escobedo tugged on the steering wheel, felt the 4x4 slide, dust streaming up from the tires. The front wheels cleared the edge of the pavement and the vehicle bounced, the hood seeming to rise in front of him. The vehicle hit the drainage ditch and dropped hard, coming to a jarring stop. Escobedo hung on to the wheel, managing to prevent himself from being thrown forward. The engine stalled and he sat in silence for a few seconds.

Move, Hermano, he thought. Before they reach you. Because you will be a dead man if they do.

He snapped out of his frozen state, pushed open the door and half fell from the car. He caught his balance and stared at his surroundings. A scrubby field swept away in front of him, and in the hazy distance he could see the edge of Broken Tree. Without a moment of hesitation, he cut across the field.

When he reached the trash-strewn back lots, Escobedo eased between two stores, emerging on the main street.

Get away from Broken Tree. The thought persisted. It was the sensible thing to do. If he remained in town, Jessup's people would find him.

He forced himself to walk calmly along the street, his mind creating and rejecting scenarios. He had to do something direct. Simple.

He walked past a bank, then suddenly stopped. To get away he would need money. He took out his wallet and used his card to draw a few hundred dollars from the bank's ATM; the money he had been saving for his future in America. With the cash in his pocket, he continued down the street.

There was a small coffee shop along the way. Escobedo went inside and ordered a drink, sat down in the farthest booth from the door, where he could still watch the street.

Had he evaded the men pursuing him?

He couldn't believe they had given up. With the realization that he had proof of Jessup's crime, they would not let up. They would search Broken Tree end to end. Probably hand out money for information about him.

He needed to do something to protect himself. He thought about going to the local police, but rejected the idea. He had heard about local law enforcement sometimes having connections with organized crime, and now that he understood Jessup's involvement with human trafficking, he couldn't fail to think along those lines. Whether it was true or not, he didn't dare expose himself to it.

Was he becoming paranoid?

He argued with himself over that. He had not imagined the events in the barn. The scene had been real. Too real. He couldn't afford to underestimate Seb Jessup.

With local law enforcement off the table, that meant going further afield.

His knowledge of the American justice system was limited. Escobedo had stayed well within the law, so had not come into contact with it, but he had heard of the FBI and Justice Department in Washington. Surely they were far enough away not to be affected by someone like Seb Jessup in a small town in Texas.

Escobedo finished his coffee and left. It was late in the afternoon. He walked through town until he came to the municipal library. It took him some time to find what he was looking for, but when he finally left, he had a telephone number written on a piece of paper.

He found a working pay phone on the edge of the park at the center of town. His hand trembled as he lifted the receiver, and he dropped a couple coins before he finally deposited the correct change.

The line was clear and the voice on the other end calm and precise. The words spoken would change Escobedo's whole life.

"Justice Department. How can I help?"

IT WAS DARK by the time Escobedo reached the building where he rented his small apartment. He stayed in the shadows, waiting until he was sure no one was watching the place, then he climbed the stairs. He let himself in quietly and used the illumination from the street to guide him around. He was not expecting to stay very long. Just enough time to stuff a few belongings into a backpack.

His instructions from the man he had spoken to in Washington had been clear: "Stay away from contact with anyone you know. Do not speak to anyone. Do exactly what the agents tell you, and cooperate. Try to behave normally, so that you do not arouse suspicions." The man had described a location, and given a time when two agents would pick him up and take him somewhere secure.

Escobedo left his apartment by the fire escape and strode quickly through the neighborhood to the rendezvous point. It was a long walk, and when he reached the spot and saw the parked SUV blink its lights, he moved faster, relieved that his pickup was waiting as promised.

He was almost at the car when the squeal of tires behind him made him glance over his shoulder. He saw the shadowy bulk of the approaching vehicle as it accelerated.

Everything moved so fast that Escobedo had no time to think of anything except staying alive.

The passenger door of the waiting car opened and an armed figure stepped out. Someone yelled for him to keep coming.

The unknown vehicle was still closing in. As it swerved across the street, automatic weapons began firing. The heavy bursts sent streams of slugs that peppered the waiting SUV and punctured the bodywork, shattering windows. The man who had stepped out of the car went down first; the driver was hit while he was still behind the wheel. Escobedo caught a brief glimpse of a bloodied face behind the windshield. The rattle of automatic fire followed him as he raced for the cover of the SUV. He had barely cleared it when a dull thud was followed by a burst of fire blossoming from the interior. He felt the heat as he swerved away from the vehicle, almost going down. The ball of flame swelled out from the car, flames curling from the bullet-shattered windows.

Escobedo saw a dark alley between two buildings and dashed into it, hiding among the shadows as he negotiated the trash-strewn pavement. When he reached a turn, he followed it and simply kept running, clutching his backpack when it slid from his shoulder.

His chest burning, Escobedo wove his way between buildings, not once looking back. He had no idea where he was going; he was just attempting to gain some distance from the shooters. He twisted around corners, ignoring the shouts of alarm as he pushed by the few people he encountered. He made no attempt to speak to them, because now he couldn't be sure who to trust.

So he trusted no one.

He was in a race for his life.

Until, exhausted, he was forced to halt. He leaned against a wall, staring around him. Struggling to breathe. Not even sure what part of town he was in. At the mouth of the alley he saw silent, dark storefronts. A deserted street. He heard distant traffic sounds. It took a few moments for him to figure out he was in a part of Broken Tree he seldom visited. Escobedo peered out from behind the building on his left and saw the lighted frontage of the bus depot a few blocks away.

The bus depot.

Could it be the answer to his problem?

Contacting the Justice Department had not worked for him. Escobedo needed another option, and he needed time to think. To plan how he was going to make this thing work. And to do that, he needed to get away from Broken Tree.

He couldn't erase what he'd seen in Jessup's barn. Despite the position he had put himself in, he knew he had to follow this through. Seb Jessup had committed murder. Escobedo had witnessed it. Recorded the very act. And his conscience would not allow him to walk away. Jessup had to pay for the brutal crime.

Escobedo also knew he was a marked man. Jessup could not afford to let the matter lie, and he was wealthy enough to pay for Escobedo's capture. His people would search for him. If Jessup got his hands on Escobedo, he'd suffer the same fate as the couple in the barn—or worse.

And then there were the two agents sent to protect him. Two more murders Escobedo had witnessed, two more dead under his watch.

He needed to get far away. Distance would grant him the time to work out what to do.

Escobedo focused on the bus depot lights again.

He would leave Broken Tree, take a coach across the border.

Into Mexico.

Back to the village where he had come from. Back home.

To Ascensión.

1

"You really believe I'm going to let that cockroach give me up to the cops?" Seb Jessup said. "I will bury that bastard and his evidence."

Three of his crew members sat in the plush office. Not one of them made any comment. They might have been thinking his outburst was more than a little risky, given that he was already under the close eye of federal authorities who were just waiting for him to step across the line.

But that was Seb Jessup.

A man who had total contempt for the law, society and anyone who dared to cross him. Jessup had a personal mantra: "I go where I want and I do what I want. Get in my way and I will crush you."

Simple and direct. Jessup believed in being up front with people. They got what they saw. He made no concessions to anyone or anything.

He was in his midthirties, a hard-bodied man who ruled his criminal organization by brute force and cunning. He had a financially successful association with a Mexican cartel over the border, and he traded in weapons and stolen cars. He also had a thriving business in human trafficking. He had no interest in corporate crime. Not for Jessup the sleight of hand in the white-collar world. He was a hands-on racketeer. Jessup liked money. Lots of it. And his territory, which still clung to the well-defined individualism of West Texas, was large enough to accommodate his appetites.

Jessup was entirely a self-made man, and he considered himself a product of his environment. Brought up on a hardscrabble farm, where his family had struggled daily to stay fed, Jessup learned early that a man got what he did only by hard work and grabbing any opportunity that presented itself. He'd made a vow that he would not end up like his folks, worn to a frazzle as they struggled to maintain some kind of life. The land they lived on was hard. The crops they grew were sparse and tended to die off if you turned your back on them.

Jessup's father was a strong man physically, but less so mentally. Each time he had a setback he would resort to the bottle, becoming surly and downright vicious. The rest of the family was often on the receiving end of Anson Jessup's hard fists. That went on until Seb's eighteenth birthday. Tired of being knocked around like a straw-filled dummy, he'd decided to fight back. He drove his bullying father to the ground, his solid fists leaving the man bloody and beaten. For the first time in his life, Jessup's simmering rage gave him the strength to overcome someone. It would not be the last time that happened.

It was his last day as part of the family. After putting his father down, he went inside the house, packed his few belongings in a bag and walked away. He never looked back.

He spent the next five years in the army. For a boy who had spent long days working the hostile land on a dirt-poor farm, army life was easy. All he had to do was follow orders, and he was given three meals a day, a bed to sleep in and a wage. When he heard other recruits grumbling about the hard life, Jessup had grinned. They knew nothing. He'd kept his head down. He was a quick learner, and he quickly gained promotion. The day he was made corporal was something he was quietly proud of.

He was eventually shipped off to the Middle East and saw a side to life he'd never even thought about back in West Texas. He witnessed killing and destruction. Experienced his first action and found himself facing the possibility of his own death. His training kicked in and he accepted that he either put it to good use or he was going to die right there and then in the midst of the dust and flies and the rattle of gunfire. He was promoted to sergeant.

He met Cole Hatton while he was in the war zone. They clicked from day one. And when the chance arose, they teamed up in a partnership that would follow into civilian life. By the time they were sent back stateside, Jessup and Hatton were considerably wealthier than when they'd first put on uniforms. The army was bringing in vast stores of goods to keep the American forces fed, clothed and armed. It was to be expected that some of those supplies would be diverted. Jessup found a way by bringing in one of the civilian contractors the military was using. Siphoned-off materials were flown back to the States, using the contract aircraft that were coming and going on an almost daily basis. Jessup started small, not wanting to attract attention, and that, coupled with the money he was pulling in from deals with the locals for food and clothing, all added to his growing cash balance.

While Jessup provided the brains, Hatton became the partnership's muscle and backup. He handled any problems that might interfere with the operations. He did it well. He was direct and dedicated, with a persuasive manner that told anyone getting in the way that it would be extremely advisable to step aside.

They set themselves up back home, building their criminal business with a dedication that would have been the envy of any hardworking entrepreneur. They operated out of a midsize community called Broken Tree, in cattle country. It was a tough town in tough borderlands.

Nine years down the road and they were established as the major player in the region. Jessup had connections across the board. He'd bought and paid for influence in high circles. He ran his organization with a hard hand and took no crap from anyone. His name opened doors, his wealth bought him the rest.

He had his world by the balls. Saw himself as untouchable. Out of reach. A big man in a big piece of country.

One of his most lucrative ventures involved bringing illegal immigrants across the border. Mexico provided plenty of people who were eager to enter the US, lured by the promise of work and money. The promises came true, though they weren't as clear-cut as the immigrants had been led to believe. Money, yes, but the expenses incurred when they were brought to America were taken from their paychecks. If they protested, they could be exposed to the authorities. That could mean jail, or being sent back to Mexico. There were times when Jessup's enforcers would hand out physical persuasion. The Mexican laborers were just another product, as far as Jessup was concerned. He bought and sold them. Had the power to make them disappear if the notion came to him. There were plenty of lonely and desolate places in border country where bodies could be, and were, made to vanish.

Jessup believed his most recent enterprise would prove to be even more lucrative. He'd met with Ramon Mariposa, the *jefe* of A La Muerte, an offshoot of the Sinaloa drug cartel. Ramon Mariposa was looking for a US distributor and Jessup had been interested in growing his presence in the drug trade.

Mariposa had learned Jessup was a solid, well-organized man who ran a thriving business, and the *jefe* also needed a steady supplier of weapons. The drug cartels were in a violent, ongoing war with competitors and Mexican law enforcement. In a brutal business, A La Muerte was way ahead of its rivals. Mariposa operated with total, unflinching violence. He saw no reason to do otherwise. His need for a reliable supply of quality ordnance was something Seb Jessup could manage easily.

In the end, it was a marriage of convenience. A two-way street. Mariposa and Jessup's relationship was beneficial to both, workable and problem free.

Until Hermano Escobedo started to rock the boat.

Rocked it with such ferocity that Jessup, for the first time since he'd faced combat, experienced fear.

He maintained his cool in front of his people, while inwardly feeling sick. Not because he was about to cave in under the threat posed by Escobedo, but because he realized for all his power, influence and wealth, he was still vulnerable. Jessup might have been resistant to threats against his security, yet he saw the shadowy possibility that his empire could be badly damaged—even brought down—by the young Mexican. Escobedo was the unexpected threat, the one coming out of left field. And he just might be capable of knocking Jessup off his throne.

Hermano Escobedo obviously felt he had justification, a good reason to strike out. Otherwise, he wouldn't have placed himself in the firing line. In truth, Jessup could even sympathize with the young man's motivation. But he still had to stop him.

If Escobedo brought his evidence into the light, Jessup could face life in prison—or even execution. He understood the penalties, and despite his position of power, realized he might conceivably pay the price.

He was going to have to play this one carefully. Hatton had broached the subject, pointing out that Jessup needed to keep his distance. No hands-on punishment this time—which pissed Jessup off. He had always been a hands-on participant. But his partner was insisting he lie low.

"We do this smart," Hatton said now. "Pull in outside help, give them the details and turn them loose."

"Not our boys?" Jessup asked.

"Nope. We stay clear. I talk to them, they keep me informed. We fund this with cash. Nothing written down, no computers—only disposable phones. Seb, we can pull this off. Take the bastard down and wipe out the evidence. With nothing to hang on you, the law is going to be pissing in the wind."

"Trouble with wind, Cole, is that it can change direction."

Hatton shook his head, a grin on his lips. "You were the only grunt who could make a joke with bullets flying over your head," he said.

"What can I say, buddy?"

Hatton levered his rangy frame out of his chair, pulling his phone from his pocket. He held it up as he walked to the door. "Today's burner," he said. "I'll make the call. Bring Candy in for a head-to-head. We'll get him on the case and set him loose on Escobedo."

"You figure that chili popper is going to make trouble, boss?" one of the remaining two crew members asked.

"He's going to try," Jessup said.

The other man said, "If Cole sets Candy on his ass, that boy isn't going to have another minute of peace. Hell, Seb, you recall when Candy went after that sucker down Nueces way? He had that done and dusted in a couple of days. No one ever found that feller's body."

"That's the way I want it with Escobedo," Jessup said. "Gone."

HATTON STOOD ON the wide porch fronting the big house, speaking into his cell.

"I want you to drop everything, Candy. This is important. Wouldn't offer it to anyone else. You sort this out for Seb and it'll be the best payday you ever had."

"He got himself in a bind?" Candy asked. His voice was low and slow, a homegrown Texas roll.

"Sort of. Candy, this needs clearing real fast. No mistakes."

"Kind that needs a shovel to finish it?"

"That kind. Dead, buried, forgotten."

"My specialty."

"The Meat Wagon in an hour. Okay?"

"Fine," Candy said, and hung up.

The Meat Wagon was a diner on the west side of Broken Tree that had been there for more than twenty-five years. The aluminum siding had weathered, the metal dull and pitted, but the painted sign had been refurbished recently. The original owner, Hoyt Dembrow, had died a few years back and the diner was managed by his son, Hoyt Dembrow Jr. Junior was over fifty and looked it, so the youthful title didn't do him any favors. The man liked the food he served in the diner, sampled it every day. His ample size showed that.

As Hatton stepped inside an hour later, the familiar smells of coffee and fried food hit him. He liked that. The Meat Wagon was a piece of stability in a rapidly changing world. It had no offshoot truck franchise, no menu with fancy food catering to dietary needs. It served American food, period, and that was the way Hatton liked it.

He spotted Candy at the back end of the diner, facing him over a raised mug of coffee. At this time of day there were only a few other customers, and Candy had picked the table farthest away, leaving an empty stretch between him and the other eaters. Hatton's boot heels clicked on the metal floor as he made his way over, stopping to speak to the owner en route.

"Hello, Junior. Coffee?"

"Sure enough, Cole."

Hatton took the offered cup and joined Candy, dropping his cowboy hat on the table beside him. Candy watched, not saying anything, as he pulled a thick envelope from his jacket and slid it across the table. Candy picked it up and lifted the flap, flipped through the thick wad of bills inside and nodded briefly.

"Down payment," Hatton said. "Usual terms."

"You paying for the food, as well?" he asked.

"Don't I always?"

Candy's lean, weathered face showed a thin smile. He was a six-foot-three whip of a man who dressed like an out-of-work line rider. He raised his hand and summoned the waitress, ordering a big steak with all the trimmings. Hatton went for his weakness: a stack of pancakes with syrup, bacon and a couple eggs on top. While they waited, Hatton pulled out some photos and showed them to Candy.

"Hermano Escobedo. Son of a bitch is ready to drop the hammer on Jessup. He has evidence that could see Jessup locked up for the rest of his life. Or worse."

"And Seb, naturally, don't sit comfortable with that."

Hatton handed over a folded sheet of paper. "Everything we have on the guy," he said. "Ain't much. He came over the border a few years back. He's legal. Set himself up doing all kinds of hands-on work. We took him on account of he's got a green thumb and does a tidy job. You know how Seb likes his place looking homey."

Candy drained his coffee and signaled for a refill. "Jessup want his body delivered—or just vanished?"

Hatton let the question hang for a few seconds.

"Hell, Candy, what would we do with a body messing up the place?"

"Just needed to clarify the situation."

"Well, it ain't hard. Find him. Put him out of his misery. Bury him in the desert and keep the shovel for a souvenir."

Candy smiled. "Hey, why'd you not say it was easy as that?"

Hatton made no comment. He knew the way Candy operated. He might make light of the deal in conversation, but in reality he was a professional who made people disappear. He gave off the impression of being a good old country boy, when he was, in fact, one of the most coldhearted men Hatton had ever come across. Candy took pride in his line of work, employed the very best and never, ever walked away without completing a contract.

They fell into light conversation until their food arrived. Eating became the most important consideration after that, neither man saying very much until they were done.

"When you catch this son of a bitch you need to look for his cell phone. He filmed Jessup. If the law lays its hands on it…"

"I get it," Candy said. "Don't you fret. It's as good as done."

"You know how to contact me if you need to," Hatton said. He finished his third coffee, pushed his plate aside and stood up. "While we were deciding how to deal with this, I set a couple of our boys on the job."

"That's fine," Candy said. "Give me the word if they find anything."

2

The call reached Mack Bolan, aka the Executioner, at Stony Man Farm. He was off mission, had been for a few days, and was beginning to wonder if the world had shut down. He knew that was a forlorn hope. Somewhere, something was happening, or about to, and he was outside the zone.

Then his phone buzzed. He picked up and heard Brognola's voice.

"Can you meet me in the War Room in five?"

There it was, then. Back to work.

Brognola nodded as Bolan entered the room. "So what do you have for me?" he asked the Big Fed.

Brognola handed over a thin file from his desk, and Bolan studied the head-and-shoulders image of a good-looking man in his early thirties, thick black hair across his forehead. There was intelligence in his dark eyes.

"Hermano Escobedo," Brognola said. "Good guy. Trying to make his way. He entered the country from

Mexico legally, sponsored by a friend. The photo is a couple years old. Escobedo lives and works in Broken Tree, West Texas."

Brognola slid another photo across his desk.

A hard face stared back at Bolan, defiance in the man's expression. Almost immediately, the soldier sensed something off-kilter.

"Seb Jessup. Texas native. Hard-ass, but smart. A spell in the army dropped him into the thick of combat in the Middle East. Army trained him to kill, and it looks like he picked up other bad habits. When he came home, he set himself up in business in Broken Tree. Built a reputation. Surrounded himself with a hard crew. Into all kinds of rackets. Soon had the money and the clout to rise to the top and stay there. Hires the best legal backing available. We know Jessup is into hard crime, but nothing's been proven. He's the bad guy in this little drama."

"What's the connection?"

"Escobedo has the goods on Jessup. Called us willing to help. Said he had hard evidence that would put Jessup behind bars, that he would hand over what he had if we could keep him alive and safe. He's no fool, Striker. Just an honest man willing to go that extra mile."

"So what happened?" Bolan asked, knowing he wouldn't have been called in if this was a simple matter of witness protection.

"Escobedo was doing some landscaping for Jessup, working in his gardens. He witnessed a pair of Mexicans, young man and woman, being beaten in one of the stables. Jessup himself was leading the attack, using a baseball bat. He was going wild. Yell-

ing about them screwing up a deal. He swore he was
going to make them an example. Escobedo told us
Jessup didn't stop until the two were dead. And he
said he caught it all on his phone."

"Bad place to be for Escobedo," Bolan said. "But
you have to give him credit. That takes courage."

Brognola nodded. "Anyway, word came to me after
the two US Marshals sent to pick him up were gunned
down. Something must have leaked after Escobedo
made the call. When backup finally got there, he was
gone. No one knows where he went. Striker, we need
you to find him. He stepped up to help and now he's
out in the cold. He's not going to trust anyone with
a shield. And he knows Jessup's people will be out
looking for him."

All Bolan had to go on was the photograph, plus
the few facts Brognola had provided. But they told
the soldier all he needed to know about Escobedo.
He was an honest man who had become a target because he had stood up to be counted. His courage
made him a threat to Seb Jessup, and men like Jessup
reacted to threats by eliminating them. Two people
had already died.

Jessup had defined the rules, so Bolan would play
by them.

It was a simple procedure. Jessup, by his actions,
had shown himself to be beyond the law. He worked
his criminal enterprises with no concern over who got
hurt. He was arrogant in his refusal to walk the line.
Bolan knew his type. He fought them every day. The
takers. The destroyers. Those who held nothing but
contempt for ordinary people. It was those *ordinary*
people Mack Bolan stood up for. They were unable

to fight back against the lawbreakers, so the Executioner did what he could to redress the balance. It was a long-term campaign, but one he accepted willingly.

Now his priority was to protect Hermano Escobedo. It was too early to assess the magnitude of the opposition. Bolan simply knew Jessup would throw a sizable force into the field. As many bodies and as much money as it would take.

Bolan was one man. That itself might work to his advantage. He had the technical resources of Stony Man as backup, but Mack Bolan was well used to his lone wolf status. It was the way he worked best. One man could move quickly, and he didn't need to wait for others to respond. He didn't have to hold back while others hesitated. Bolan went in at his own speed, making his decisions on the go, and there were no rules of engagement to consider. If something needed doing he simply went ahead and did it.

"Hal, bring Jack in. I'm going to need a ride to Texas."

Ascensión, Chihuahua, Mexico

DRY AND DUSTY wind blew in from the open land beyond town. Hermano Escobedo felt the gritty detritus patter against his clothing as he walked the quiet street and ducked his head against the persistent dust. It was the time of day when sensible people stayed indoors to wait out the heat of the afternoon and take a siesta. Escobedo allowed a faint smile to curl his mouth at the thought.

Sensible people.

People with no worries except what to make for dinner and the price of gas.

But he was not like them. The days of normality were far behind him. Now he was a man alone, forced to turn his back on his few friends for fear of drawing trouble to them—or finding out they weren't such trustworthy friends, after all. Escobedo knew what could happen if one of Jessup's men found out someone knew too much. So he spoke to no one and made his plans to leave the area. He did this carefully, but he understood the way his enemy worked. Jessup had secretive ways of sniffing people out, using his money and the men who worked for him. If they located Escobedo, his life would not be worth very much.

The US Department of Justice had promised him protection. That he would be safe under their watchful eye. He had believed them, trusted in their competence to do what they'd promised. And at first it seemed to have been working. But then everything changed.

His protectors had failed him. Not only that, but they had forfeited their lives.

He'd escaped with his own, but now he was an open target. He had made the fatal mistake of threatening to expose Seb Jessup.

Escobedo knew enough about his former employer to understand he had so much influence and money, so many people in his pocket, that even thinking about going up against him was like peeing on an oil rig fire. It was a gesture. Nothing more. The man would hound him. Push him around and stall any effort to make his accusations stick. Already Escobedo had been thrown to the wolves. His contact with the law had been severed. Two men were dead and he was isolated.

So he walked away. From his friends. From his home. From everything that could be connected to him.

He had taken a crowded bus into Mexico. An old vehicle with tired suspension, it had bounced over every rough spot in the road. He'd endured the dusty, noisy ride in silence. When the coach reached its destination, Escobedo grabbed his backpack and climbed out, then bought a ticket that would take him deeper into the country. The coach he boarded this time was even older. There was no glass in the windows and as soon as the vehicle chugged onto the potholed local road, dust drifted inside. The seat under him was poorly padded and oily fumes from the engine filtered up through the rusty floor.

Escobedo opened one of the plastic bottles of water he had bought, and took a mouthful. He sat back, channeling out the noise, and tried, unsuccessfully, to relax.

He did not fool himself into believing that once he'd crossed that border he would be completely safe. But he believed he'd have some advantage on home turf. He'd be better able to lose himself in a country he knew intimately than he would in the US. Here he could melt into the background.

That was his hope, though already he was considering the validity of the moves he was making.

He stared out the bus window, seeing only the dry landscape.

Escobedo checked carefully each time the bus stopped to let off passengers or take on new ones. He scanned the other riders for anyone who stood out, but saw only the expected locals. Still, he couldn't relax fully. He couldn't rid himself of the suspicion Jessup might already have his people in place.

The village appeared out of the haze. Escobedo knew it well. In the years he had been gone, very little had changed. The tired buildings, the uneven road. At one time he'd called this place home.

It was Ascensión.

The town he had left to go to America. And like many pilgrims who walked away, he was now returning, because in his time of trouble he could think of nowhere else to go.

The village square still housed the stone fountain surrounded by skinny trees. There were no new buildings, just the familiar, whitewashed ones he remembered. As Escobedo stepped off the bus, memories came flooding back. He settled his backpack and walked across the square to the church as the bus disappeared in a cloud of dust.

Escobedo stopped at the base of the worn stone steps that led inside.

How long since he had been inside a church?

Too long.

Now he hesitated outside the house of God and wondered exactly what he was doing there.

He paused for a second too long. About to walk away, he was disturbed by the deep voice that spoke to him from the shadows just inside the open door.

"Hermano Escobedo? Yes, it is you."

Father Xavier stepped into the sunlight, arms extended. His creased brown face held an expression of delight as he looked down at Escobedo. He must be in his seventies now, but to Escobedo the priest had changed little over the years. He wore the brown robe and sandals he always had. He was a man of medium height, lean and agile, a man who reveled in his chosen calling and was imbued with an inexhaustible energy.

He reached out to Escobedo and embraced him, holding him close for a while.

"You remember me so easily?" Escobedo said.

"Mano, I would be failing in my calling if I could not recognize one of my flock."

"Even after so many years? After I walked away from the church?"

Xavier smiled. "My son, because you have strayed from the path, God does not abandon you."

"Still the persuasive words."

"Mano, I have been doing this a long time. And by your tone I suspect you have much on your mind." Xavier made a welcoming gesture with one hand. "Come inside so we can talk."

Escobedo found himself following the priest. As he passed through the open doors he felt the silent calm reach out to blanket him. Felt the coolness within.

Father Xavier led him past the pews, pausing at the altar, then turned and headed to the rear of the church, where he had his living quarters.

"Nothing seems to have changed," Escobedo said as he stood in the doorway. "It's like I have never been away." He paused then, guilt rising as he recalled something he had half forgotten. "Father, I ask forgiveness for not thanking you for what you did for my grandparents. How you arranged to have them buried, and let me know."

"You sent me a letter in reply."

"It was too little and too late."

"But you did *not* forget. That is the important part."

"Father…I…"

"Sit down, Mano," Xavier said.

Escobedo slipped off his backpack and took a seat, watching as Xavier busied himself at the simple stove, boiling water to make coffee. He handed Escobedo a cup, took one himself and sat across from the younger man.

"Your journey here now has to be more than a simple desire to return to your home," he said. "It has to be something important to bring you all the way back from America."

"Perhaps I just wanted to make a visit."

"Mmm." Xavier nodded. "But something more than that, I feel." He sipped his coffee.

"You're right, Father. I came because I needed somewhere to hide." Escobedo stared at him. "It was not in my heart to seek absolution. Or to burden you with my problems…"

"But when you saw the church, the old feelings drew you here." Xavier smiled. "It is well known the church embraces those who seek comfort. Whether they believe they need it or not." He paused. "Is that not so, Mano?"

Escobedo drank more of his coffee and allowed his thoughts to assemble in some kind of order. Then he told him what he had seen and the danger he now faced.

"And do these men have guns?" the priest asked.

"*Sí.*"

"And do you, Mano, have a gun with which to defend yourself?"

"No, Father. I have nothing. I am not a man of violence."

"Then you did the only thing you could, and walked away from these people."

"I could not think of anything else I could do."

"A wise move. Now, will you stay here? Or move on? This I ask only so that I can make some arrangements."

Escobedo shrugged. "The last thing I wish is to bring my problems to you."

"Do you believe these people may come here?"

"It's possible. I've been selfish and thoughtless. I thought coming here would put me out of their reach, but that was stupid of me. I need to go. Move on before people get hurt because of me."

"You will do no such thing, Mano. Let me think about this. I am sure we can figure out something."

"Ascensión is small. The people here can do nothing against these men. I will only bring trouble."

"Then we must get you far away. To a place where even these people cannot find you. Trust me, Hermano. I have a good friend. A priest who has a church in a small village much like Ascensión. It's by the ocean, below Culiacán. There you can have the time to decide what you must do."

"This could be dangerous for you, Father Xavier. Too dangerous."

"Let me worry about that. Mano, it may take me a few days to arrange this. Until it is time to go you will need to remain as out of sight as possible."

"I could go the family farm. Now my grandparents are both dead, I'll be alone there."

"Good. I will send for you when everything is ready. I can get you food, and old Quilla can lend me a burro." Xavier smiled. "Have you remembered how to ride one?"

For the first time in many days Escobedo smiled. "Ride a burro? Father, it is something you never forget."

"Then it is settled, Mano. Take some more coffee and I will go and get things ready for you."

3

Broken Tree, Texas

Mack Bolan studied the apartment building from the confines of his car, checking out the area around it and not moving until he felt secure. The building stood on a quiet street, away from the main drag. It wasn't exactly a poor area of town, but the homes were not likely to be featured in any upmarket style magazines. Hermano Escobedo lived well within his pay grade.

After glancing at his watch, Bolan decided it was time to move. He had the location of Escobedo's rooms, and though he doubted the man was home, he had to start his search somewhere.

He exited his vehicle and locked it, then checked his Beretta 93R in its shoulder holster. He wore civilian clothing—a light shirt under his jacket, tan chinos and soft-soled shoes. The area was quiet. Bolan stepped inside the building and made his way to the rear stairs, up to Escobedo's floor. He could hear voices, speaking mainly in Spanish; the yell of a playing child. Faint music came from behind a closed door. He walked along the hallway and stopped at Escobedo's apartment. There were slight indentations around the edge of the door level with the catch, the damaged wood showing fresh marks.

Bolan slid his hand inside his leather jacket and gripped the Beretta 93R. He slid the autopistol free and held it down by his right side as he gently eased the unlocked door open, just enough to slip through.

He was in a short hall that ran the length of the apartment, with a pair of doors branching off left and right ahead of him. He heard activity coming from the room to his left, then voices.

"…wasting our time. Escobedo isn't here and anything he had he took with him."

"Hell, man, you don't know that."

"If he was smart enough to bug out he won't have left us a message."

Something banged on the floor.

"Why don't you just yell and let the neighbors know we're in here."

"Okay, okay."

"We don't come up with anything, someone is going to be pissed."

"The hell with that. If there isn't anything to find, what are we supposed to do? Get creative and make something up? Face it, Clegg, he's gone."

"Candy likes answers."

"Yeah? I like college girls. How many times do I get them?"

Bolan eased up to the doorway of the occupied room and peered inside.

It was sparsely furnished, with a faded carpet, and an old TV set in one corner. Walls that were once cream had lost their color.

And there were two men. Jeans and boots, baggy shirts. One had a curl-brimmed Stetson pushed to the back of his head. He also had an autopistol tucked down the back of his Levi's.

They were going through a cheap sideboard, scattering the contents of the drawers across the floor. In frustration, one of the men pushed a row of books off a shelf.

"No goddam phone left here," the one called Clegg said.

"If he had stuff on it for the cops, there ain't no chance he'd leave it here."

"And Hermano keeps the place so tidy," Bolan said, quietly announcing his presence. "I hope you're thinking of cleaning up."

The pair turned in concert, the one with the waistbanded pistol snaking a hand around to grasp it.

"Who the hell are you?"

"Obviously not your best friend," Bolan said, raising the 93R.

He turned toward the guy with the gun, so the other man took his chance, bunching his shoulders as he launched himself across the short distance. His left hand jerked up, showing the lock knife he held. The blade snapped into place as he closed in on the soldier, but he failed to notice Bolan's hand as he swept it around and slammed the butt of the Beretta against his nose. Hard. Then a second time. The guy's nose simply collapsed under the stunning impact. Blood gushed from his nostrils and he stumbled, dropping his knife.

Bolan didn't hesitate to swing the 93R back around to his second target. The Beretta was set for triple fire and he laid three suppressed 9 mm slugs into the guy's chest. He struck the wall, his face registering shock. His legs gave way and he slid down the plaster, giving off a long sigh.

A soft probe had turned hard. It wasn't the first time Bolan had been confronted with unexpected hostility, and the situation had called for rapid action. If he had been a fraction slower it might easily have been him down on the floor, and anyone who raised a violent hand in the Executioner's direction had to be dealt with.

A scrabbling sound reached Bolan's ears and he turned. The first guy was lunging for the knife he'd dropped. Bolan had not had the time to clear the blade, and as the man clenched the weapon in his fist Bolan moved forward to intercept, stomping on his opponent's outstretched fingers. Bone crunched and a pained yell burst from the guy's mouth. Bolan had already followed through, his other foot arcing around and smashing into the side of the man's exposed throat. A strangled grunt escaped the already bloody lips as his head snapped to one side. He rolled over, landing hard, and the way he sprawled told Bolan his blow had broken the guy's neck.

The soldier turned aside, aware that any time he might have had in Escobedo's apartment was running out. He had no way of knowing whether the intruders had partners close by, maybe watching out while their buddies searched the place. He needed to complete his own search quickly, and move on.

Bolan's first chore was to check the two men to see if they'd been carrying anything useful. All he turned up was one cell phone, which he pocketed. Next, he examined the rooms. The flimsy wardrobe in the bedroom contained only empty wire hangers. Bolan realized Escobedo must have taken every item of clothing he owned; which suggested he was not anticipating a return. The same went for personal belongings. It looked as if Hermano Escobedo had cleared the apartment.

Back in the living room, Bolan crouched down and went through the few items that had been strewn across the floor. A few magazines, old newspapers, paperback books. As he rifled through them, something slipped out from between the pages of one volume. A creased photograph showed a view of what appeared to be a Mexican village. A town square with a fountain, and a church on the far side. There were a few lines of writing on the back, too faded for Bolan to read. He turned the picture over again and studied the image.

Just a street in some distant Mexican village. But he'd ask Aaron Kurtzman and his team at Stony Man to run it through the system.

Bolan spent another fruitless ten minutes going through the apartment. He found nothing else, so left as quietly as he had arrived, through to the rear of the building and across the back lot, taking a slow, circuitous route to where he had left his vehicle. He drove away, heading back to where he had left Grimaldi waiting with the plane, at an airstrip about an hour out of Broken Tree.

Bolan had established that someone *was* looking for Hermano Escobedo, and not to invite him for a quiet drink. If there was an intensive search taking place, on top of the deaths of the two marshals, then Seb Jessup did have something to hide.

Bolan had been tasked with finding Escobedo and bringing him in alive. Now he knew he was in a race against Jessup's people. That knowledge did nothing to deter him. He would search for and find Escobedo. Once the Executioner took up the challenge he would not be persuaded to step aside. Especially not when he was there to protect the life of a hounded man.

4

Broken Tree, Texas

"Somebody is interested in Escobedo's whereabouts," Bolan said into his sat phone. "Enough to put their lives on the line."

"I don't like the sound of that," Brognola said.

"They made the choice," Bolan said, detailing what had happened at Escobedo's apartment. "Couple of things I'd like Bear to check for me."

"Go ahead."

"I have a picture I'm sending through from my cell. I need the cyber boys to see if they can identify the printing on the rear. See if they can tell me where the photo was taken. It's a long shot, but right now I don't have much else to go on except a name. One of the guys in Escobedo's apartment used it. Candy. Thin, I know, but maybe we can tie this guy to Jessup."

"Okay," Brognola said. "Call you back if we get anything. You got any thoughts on this?"

"I'm thinking—guessing—that Escobedo has jumped the border, gone into Mexico to lose himself. He stays on this side, he's in Jessup's backyard. He'd be less conspicuous in his own country, and he might already know a place to hide."

"So maybe the photo is somewhere familiar to Escobedo?"

"Could be, Hal. The guy moved to the US to work. Left his home behind. Could be the photo holds memories for him. A reminder. People like to keep things like that."

"We'll go with that for now," Brognola said. "Like you say, we don't have much else. You hanging on to Jack?"

"No. He can make his way back. I'll collect my gear from the plane and get a room in a local motel. If Aaron comes up with anything I can decide what to do from there. I'm sending a cell along with Grimaldi. Took it from one of the intruders. There might be something useful in its memory. And I'll send my Beretta with Jack, too. If I'm crossing the border I can't risk carrying. Pointless to have my weapon with me if I get caught up in a search by the authorities."

"I can let a couple of my men know what happened in Broken Tree," Brognola said. "If there's any local problem, they can run an overwatch. Cover your back if the you-know-what hits the fan."

"I don't want to be a killjoy," Bolan said, "but tell them to walk softly in case this Jessup character has any connections with the local law."

AN HOUR AFTER Grimaldi took off, Bolan was in the diner attached to the motel he had located a few miles down the highway. A welcome sight for any traveler negotiating the long and lonely Texas road. Bolan was on his second coffee when his phone rang.

"Hey, cowboy, how is it down there in the Lone Star State?"

The voice was familiar and welcome, clear and sharp over the satellite connection.

"All the more *lone* without you here," Bolan said.

"Why do I never have my voice recorder handy when you say things like that?" Barbara Price's tone was easy and friendly.

"Remind me when I get back to say it again. But right now, I take it you've got something for me?"

"We have some information Bear believes will be of help."

"Go ahead."

"The picture from your phone has the photographer's logo on the rear. Pretty faded, but by the magic of computer enhancement our guys worked at the pixels and enhanced them until they were readable."

"What do we have?"

"We're looking at the town of Ascensión. The photo shows the square and the church on the Avenida de la Ascensión. I'm sending you the enhanced image. And a location for the town."

"Tell Aaron and the team thanks. I've got a starting point now."

"Anything else you need at the moment?"

"I sent my Beretta back with Jack. Didn't want to risk being caught trying to take a firearm across the border."

"Lucky for you we have some sources available. I'll make a call and speak with you once you've made the crossing. Do I need to tell you to take care?"

"You always do."

"Watch yourself, soldier."

They ended the call there. Bolan finished his coffee and made his way to his room. The data had come through from Stony Man and Bolan studied the sharpened image. Kurtzman had also sent some GPS coordinates that gave Bolan a starting point from the border crossing a few miles from Broken Tree. He brought up a map of the route to Ascensión. It was a day and a half's journey, and would take Bolan into isolated territory. He could understand if this was where Escobedo had traveled, and the more he thought about it, the more likely it seemed that the fugitive had headed home. Rural Mexico. Off the beaten track. Burdened with information he would not have chosen to have, Hermano Escobedo had likely retreated to familiar ground, searching for anonymity. Bolan had a suspicion the man might not be as successful as he hoped.

The soldier checked the gear he had brought with him from Stony Man. For a cover, he had taken on the guise of a freelance photographer on assignment. Stony Man had a dummy publication that would back him up if anyone should look into his credentials. The business cards he carried had him down as Mark Lassiter, and Bolan had the necessary documents and US passport to confirm his identity. Lassiter's trip to Mexico was for the purpose of photographing landscapes and buildings to be featured in an upcoming spread of a travel magazine. With her usual efficiency and speed, Barbara Price had pulled together the package, handing it to Bolan just before he had moved out with Grimaldi.

Plugging his sat phone into its charger, the soldier turned in for the night. He had a long drive ahead of him in the morning.

BOLAN WOKE BEFORE dawn and ate a light breakfast before loading his belongings into his 4x4. He drove to the rental agency and paid to extend the rental period, making sure the gas tank was filled and the oil and water levels topped up.

He reached the border crossing by midmorning and waited in line to enter Mexico.

His thoughts went back to Hermano Escobedo's apartment and the dead men he had left there. The radio he had tuned in to, a local station, made no mention of the bodies. It was possible they had not yet been discovered. There were other possibilities. Brognola might have exercised Federal influence to have news of the deaths suppressed in order to leave Bolan in the clear and give him time to get into Mexico. The chance that Jessup's own persuasive power might also have been working crossed Bolan's mind. If the man imagined some outside agency was working on Escobedo's disappearance, he might have kept the deaths quiet so his own search for the Mexican could proceed without too much external interference.

Bolan passed through the border crossing with no problems. It was a busy day and the guards on both sides had enough on their hands to be concerned about a harmless American photographer on his way to take pictures. After his papers were checked, he was sent on his way.

5

Broken Tree, Texas

Candy leaned against the weathered fence and watched as one of his hands worked on an unbroken mustang. The animal had plenty of fight in him, kicking and fishtailing his way around the dusty corral. Despite the animal's brute strength, the man in the saddle refused to quit. He was Candy's best bronco buster; a bowlegged, sun-dried cowboy who didn't understand the word *quit*. He would, if need be, cling to that saddle for the whole damn day.

"We got the word," someone said behind Candy.

He turned and saw one of his men, Lorenzo, standing close by.

"Hope it's the word I want to hear."

"Tye and Clegg were pulled out of Escobedo's place. Both dead. Hatton told me he'll make sure they won't be found."

"What about the son of a bitch who took 'em down?"

"Single guy who went into Escobedo's building. He left by the back door. When the backup went in they found the two dead hombres. They got a look at the guy who left and a description of his wheels. Plate numbers. We circulated the information. I got a call from Rodriguez at the border crossing. The guy went through, heading into Mexico."

"Hatton played it smart, having someone stand watch." Candy took the makings from his shirt pocket and rolled a smoke. "Wonder what the guy found to send him across the border."

Lorenzo shrugged. "Whoever he is, this boy is no amateur."

"I'll make a call."

Candy set off for the main house across the ranch yard. He went to his office, where he perched on the edge of his desk and picked up an unused burn phone, tapping in a number he knew from memory.

"*Hola, amigo. ¿Cómo estás?*" he said.

The man at the other end laughed. "You know, my friend," he said in English, "your Spanish gets no better."

"Ramon, you are not wrong there."

"So what can I do for you? There has to be more than an excuse for you to practice your terrible Spanish."

"I need a little help with a problem."

Lorenzo, who had followed Candy inside, listened as he spoke. The moment Candy greeted Ramon, concern etched Lorenzo's face. Candy saw him staring, and grinned.

He was speaking with Ramon Mariposa, the head of A La Muerte.

Mariposa listened in silence until Candy finished explaining the situation.

"This Escobedo could make problems if his information passes into the hands of the law. If Jessup comes under close examination, it could expose our connection. I wouldn't like that, Candy."

"Well, hell, son, Jessup isn't too pleased, either," Candy said. "Ramon, we're pretty sure Escobedo is back on home turf. So this guy following him must be in Mexico, too."

"Then we need to find them both. This American could be our lead to Escobedo."

"I'll come on down to you," Candy said. "Give you guys a hand. That okay with you, *amigo*?"

"Of course. I have always been in favor of cross-border cooperation."

"This willingness to cooperate couldn't be shaded with self-preservation, would it?"

Mariposa laughed. "My friend, you paint a very dim picture of me."

"Son, don't forget I know you too well."

"Yes, you do. I look forward to seeing you soon. Then we can go hunt these cockroaches."

"Listen," Candy said. "I'll text you what we have on this yahoo. Vehicle make and registration. Give you a chance to have some of your boys pick up his trail."

"I'll have a crew ready to go. There is only one road he can come along in this area. I have no doubt my men will find him."

6

Chihuahua, Mexico

A couple hours into his drive, Bolan heard his sat phone and picked up.

"There's a village coming up in about ten miles," Price told him. "Your guy will be waiting in a vintage Buick. Dark blue. Whitewall tires and lots of chrome. There's a cantina on your right when you reach the center of the village. I'm looking at it in real time via the satellite cameras. Looks like a pleasant little village. I'll have Aaron stay on so we can see you make the contact. Your guy is a Mexican, name of Pablo Gutierrez. You'll find this next piece of information interesting. Gutierrez was a business contact of the late Jack Regan. You remember Regan?"

Regan had been an arms dealer who had crossed paths with the Stony Man teams on a number of occasions. Jack "Bubba" Regan had carved a niche for himself in the trade of illegal weapons, ready to sell to anyone who could show him ready money. Sides didn't matter to him, just the payoff. Over time, he had traded with both sides of the coin in the US and worldwide. Good and bad. Until the day a deal went sour on him and he was killed in the middle of a firefight.

"Not likely to forget him," Bolan said, recalling the day Regan had died. The soldier had been there on a mission.

"Then you won't mistake Gutierrez," Price said. "He'll be parked near the cantina. And he'll identify himself with a password."

"Thanks for the heads-up, Miss Price. Much appreciated." They ended the call.

Eventually, Bolan picked out the outline of the village through the thermal ripples bridging the road. There was a gas station, a couple stores. The cantina. A few well-used vehicles parked irregularly along the street.

The described American gas-guzzler stood alongside the cantina. A thin film of dust lay over the paint job and the chrome accessories. He noticed the whitewall tires looked pristine. Not a mark or stain on the rubber.

And leaning against the driver's side door was the guy Price had named as Gutierrez. Lean and hollow-cheeked, the man was on the short side. The brim of his Panama hat shielded eyes that tracked Bolan's movements as he parked and stepped out of the 4x4.

"Cooper?" The voice was surprisingly soft, the Mexican accent strong.

Bolan nodded. "Gutierrez?" The Panama hat

bobbed up and down. Bolan said, "You're making a delivery."

"Only for a special customer."

The passwords exchanged, Gutierrez turned and leaned inside the car, lifting out a black duffel bag. He passed it to Bolan.

"You wish to check it? Only I have a long drive back and need to go."

Bolan could feel the solid weight of the contents. He unzipped the bag and quickly peered inside. Satisfied, he closed it up. "Looks good. *Gracias.*"

Gutierrez said nothing more. He climbed into the Buick and fired up the engine, made a U-turn and headed back along the highway. Bolan drove to the gas station and topped up the 4x4's tank, then rolled back onto the road and kept going. His sat phone rang. It was Price again.

"You could have waved," she said.

"That would be a giveaway if I'm being watched."

"You *are* being watched, Striker."

"I meant by other than you."

"Another ten minutes and you'll be out of range."

"I'll miss you."

"Aaron has loaded the satnav route onto your phone, so you can't miss Ascensión," Price said. "Stay safe, Striker."

Bolan pulled over on the side of the empty road. He opened the duffel and lifted out the hardware, checking the contents.

A Beretta 92FS with 9 mm Parabellum and a 15-round mag capacity. A pistol Bolan was familiar with, though he would have preferred the 93R. Gutierrez had included four additional magazines. The pistol was not new, but looked well maintained. There were also four 40-round magazines for the Uzi SMG in the bag, plus one already loaded in the weapon. Bolan had used the Israeli SMG on countless missions and was more than comfortable with the hardware. The duffel also contained a shoulder rig for the Beretta and a sheathed Cold Steel Tanto knife.

Bolan took the 92FS out of the bag and placed it in the glove box, where he could reach it quickly. He pushed the duffel beneath the front passenger seat, then took a few of the cameras out of his luggage and placed them on the seat next to him. He was hoping there would not be any need to cover himself, but he was aware of his unofficial presence in Mexico and the complications that might present. Going undercover was always a risky proposition, placing him way outside the law.

He fired up the engine and swung the 4x4 back onto the road. He drove at a steady speed, focusing on what lay ahead. If he failed to reach Escobedo before Jessup's crew did, the Mexican's life could be forfeit.

Mack Bolan had operated in the wilderness for a long time. His chosen way of life was a one-man crusade against the evil side of humanity. He battled for Justice, without a waving flag or flowery rhetoric. He simply sided with the people who had no way to fight back against corruption and violence. Against men who saw the world as their cake and wanted to devour every last morsel. Bolan stood in their path and waged a never-ending war.

He understood his limitations. The immense struggle to stem the tide.

He did it because someone had to.

He did it because he could.

Glancing in his rearview mirror, Bolan realized a car was following him.

As far as he knew, this was one of the few roads in the area, so he'd expected to see other traffic. But this vehicle was acting strangely, hanging back an odd distance. Unless the driver was cruising, in no hurry to get anywhere, he could be staying at a safe distance from Bolan's 4x4 on purpose.

The soldier had no idea how it had happened, but it seemed the opposition had tagged him. Seb Jessup's organization was proving to be more than good. If nothing else, this showed Bolan that he was up against an enemy that could already be a few steps ahead of him.

He wondered how much they knew. If Jessup already had wind of Escobedo's whereabouts, why would they need to tail Bolan? They must be letting him lead them to their target.

In any case, he had their company and needed to get them off his back. On the open road, he was unlikely to outrun them. He wasn't going to buy them off. His only option would be to prevent them from following him.

Bolan's gaze dropped briefly to the edge of the duffel under the passenger seat. The Uzi should have the capability to dissuade them. Its powerful rate of fire would inflict damage to the trailing vehicle—and also to the men riding in it, if that was needed. He reached down and dragged the bag clear, unzipping it. Bolan eased the Uzi out and dropped it across his lap. He flipped the selector to full-auto.

A quick check in the mirror showed him the vehicle was still following, maintaining its distance. He looked ahead and saw a rise in the road, where it followed the contours of the land—a natural ridge that crossed from west to east, stringing out for miles on either side. The moment Bolan dropped beyond the crest he would be out of sight until his pursuers reached the top, a few minutes later. As a plan, it was thin. But Bolan had worked similar bluffs before, and it would give him a slim window of opportunity. If the vehicle was not, in fact, following him, it would continue on its way. If it was, his pursuers would have to effect a rapid response. And within that narrow time frame Bolan would be offered his chance.

7

"He has vanished," Julio Prieto said, leaning forward to stare out the dusty windshield. "How can he disappear on such a straight road?"

Renaldo Calvera smacked the back of Prieto's head. "He hasn't vanished, you idiot. He has gone over the rise ahead. Just keep driving."

From the rear of the big SUV, the third man, Tito Villas, said, "Listening to you two is like being with children. It's a good thing Mariposa can't hear you. He sent us to find this Escobedo and deal with the American looking for him. So shut up and do it."

"We are, Villas," Calvera said. "Just pass out the guns and stop being a pain."

The three men from A La Muerte were well armed. They carried a selection of handguns and automatic weapons. Their orders were simple, coming directly from Ramon Mariposa. They were to find the runaway, Hermano Escobedo, and make sure he would not be alive to offer his evidence to *norteamericano* law enforcement. The request had come via Mariposa's American compadre, Candy. It was a simple one, a favor between friends. Candy himself would be traveling across the border to see that the assignment was carried out to his satisfaction. The trio from A La Muerte was going ahead to make sure Escobedo did not become lost again. Once they had located him, they would take out the American, as well.

Prieto pushed his foot down on the gas pedal, anxious to get over the rise so they could keep their eyes on the other vehicle. The SUV sped over the crest, swaying as it hit the downside.

"*Dios*," Prieto said. "I told you he had gone."

The road ahead appeared to be empty. No vehicle. No lingering dust in the air.

Prieto stomped on the brake. The SUV burned rubber as it swerved from side to side. In truth, Prieto was not a very good driver. He wrestled with the wheel as the car slithered along the slope.

"There. *There*," Calvera yelled. "He's at the side of the road."

The SUV came to a swaying stop broadside across the pavement, and as they stared out the windows they saw the 4x4 parked on the shoulder, facing them. The driver was standing beside it.

And he was holding a weapon.

Villas snatched up handguns from the seat beside him and thrust one into Calvera's hands. He practically threw a cut-down shotgun at Prieto.

Calvera kicked open his door and tumbled out, then scrambled around to the rear of the SUV. Prieto and Villas exited together and brought their weapons to bear on the waiting man.

It was Prieto who fired first, triggering a round hastily. The charge blew harmlessly wide of its intended target, a reckless move that was about to have serious repercussions for the trio.

The American barely appeared to move as the dark configuration of his weapon arced toward them. Then he began to shoot, flame winking from the muzzle as the gun jacked out a rapid burst of autofire. Prieto gave a squeal of terror as a number of slugs hammered at his chest. He was pushed back against the open door of the SUV, more of the slugs shattering the window behind him.

Even before Prieto went down, the American had dropped to a crouch and lined up the barrel of his weapon with Villas, catching him as he triggered his automatic pistol. The stream of bullets caught Villas across his right shoulder, knocking him sideways so that the burst chopped at his arm and side. He slid back across the rear seat, spattering it with his blood and fragments of flesh as he fell. A second burst burrowed under his jaw, angling up through his head to lodge in his brain.

Calvera heard the bursts of fire. He was already cutting around the rear of the SUV, his pistol clutched tightly in his right hand. He ducked below the window level, heart pounding as he heard Prieto scream. Things were going badly. But he had committed himself, and as a loyal A La Muerte soldier, he could not back away. He thrust the pistol ahead of him as he rounded the vehicle, searching for a target. He spotted the crouching American as he put Villas down. Calvera jerked his pistol in that direction, finger pulling back on the trigger.

In the fraction of time between firing and realizing he had been too slow, Calvera saw the mistakes that had been made. Prieto had committed them to action too quickly. His first shot had laid out what was going to happen before he had thought about it. They had been following the American so he might lead them to Escobedo. Too eager to make the first move, Prieto had gone ahead on his own, and once he had done that there was no going back. Now Prieto and Villas were injured, maybe even dead, and Calvera himself was in that transition between success and failure...

He completed his trigger pull, saw the muzzle of his pistol rise as it fired. As the weapon discharged, he felt hard thumps against the chest, multiple strikes, and he felt himself falling backward under the impact. He rolled against the SUV, numbness flowing through his body. He had been shot. He slid to his knees, his free hand groping for some kind of support, but there was nothing to hold on to. Calvera hit the ground hard, thinking Mariposa was going to be angry because they had messed up...

He coughed and tasted blood in his mouth, warm and brassy. His senses were fading and the only clear thought he acknowledged was that at least he had stayed true to the code.

A la muerte.

To the death.

BOLAN HELD HIS POSITION as he saw the third shooter fall, sprawling on the road behind the SUV. The pistol he had carried spilled from his hand as he relaxed in death. Rising to his feet, Bolan checked the other pair. Neither moved from where they had fallen. Their weapons lay on the ground near their bodies. Bolan approached cautiously; it was not unknown for men to make a final move after faking death. He had no intention of being caught by a trick like that.

He went from man to man, kicking away dropped weapons, then gathering them from a safe distance. He paused briefly to confirm that his shots had been fatal. He took out his sat phone and photographed each body, then sent the images to Stony Man with a brief request for identification.

Jessup was obviously playing a hard game. The man was pushing for a result, and that meant Bolan needed to be on his toes. What had happened here told him he could expect more.

He returned to his vehicle, placed the Uzi on the seat beside him and the dead men's weapons in the duffel, and drove away.

Back on the road, Bolan watched for any further signs of pursuit, both ahead and behind. He saw nothing over the course of an hour.

He finally made out the formation of buildings ahead, emerging from the heat haze. It was early evening. He still had a good distance to travel before reaching Ascensión, and needed to touch base with Stony Man, so decided to take a short break.

As Bolan pulled up beside a small taqueria, his sat phone buzzed. He checked the message. It was from Aaron Kurtzman.

A positive identification had been made of one of the dead men. The information had come from a DEA file on a gang operating out of Chihuahua—A La Muerte, an offshoot of a major drug cartel.

The man was Renaldo Calvera, a soldier who worked under Ramon Mariposa. Mariposa was a drug lord who ran a wide territory all the way up to the border. Kurtzman had included additional information on the man, gathered from multiple agencies.

Bolan scanned the data and the accompanying images attached, which showed a number of A La Muerte members. They included both the other men he had shot, as well as the head honcho himself. Bolan committed Mariposa's image to memory.

The soldier sent a text asking if there was a link between Mariposa and Seb Jessup. Kurtzman confirmed that there was. The DEA had evidence that the two men had done business together over a number of years. Drugs one way, weapons the other. A pairing of like minds.

Neither operation had been affected by the scrutiny of the law. They were insulated by their lawyers and the simple fact that no one had the courage to go against them. To stand up against Jessup and the Mexican cartel would put any individual on the execution block. Which made Hermano Escobedo an exceptional man.

What Jessup and now Mariposa would need to know was that the man searching for Escobedo was beyond their influence. Nothing they could say or do would deter him.

The Executioner could not be intimidated.

He would seek his enemies and destroy them if they stood in his way.

No hesitation.

No mercy.

No second chance.

8

Chihuahua

The second the plane wheels stopped turning, Candy opened the side door, activated the steps and walked onto the strip. He saw Ramon Mariposa moving to meet him. Behind the Mexican was the black Hummer he always traveled in, and on his heels were two casually dressed, well-armed bodyguards. Over-the-top security like that always made Candy smile. He had come to Mexico alone, his only protection holstered on his hip. He supposed he could understand Mariposa's caution, though. In the drug business, there was always someone plotting a coup. The vast wealth the industry generated created envy, greed and a lust for power. The law was just one hindrance to Mariposa. The bigger threat was from rivals. Those with eyes on his wealth and his operation.

Still, if someone wanted to take Mariposa down, he could do it from a safe distance with a good rifle.

The armed escorts flanking Mariposa would have no way to prevent an attack coming out of left field. As good as they were, they couldn't do a great deal to stop an assassin who made his play unannounced. Candy figured if someone was out to hit you and had a lick of sense, he would figure out a way. And Candy had decided long ago that he was big enough to look after himself. As long as he had his gun with him, he would do what needed to be done.

"Hey, amigo," he said.

Mariposa nodded. It was easy to see he was not in a happy state of mind. Candy could understand that. Three of his men blown away before they had a chance to make any kind of headway. That would have hurt Mariposa as much as a bullet to the brain.

Ramon Mariposa cut an imposing figure. He was tall, broad in the shoulders, slim in the hips. In his midthirties, he had handsome features and his thick, dark hair shone with health, almost reaching the collar of his expensive suit. It was black, as was the open-neck silk shirt he wore under it. He favored hand-tooled, Western-style boots, the leather embossed with an intricate design. Mariposa enjoyed flaunting the wealth his narcotics business made for him. Candy knew the man carried a SIG-Sauer P226 in a snug holster on his right hip, hidden by his beautifully cut jacket.

The loss of his men was something he would have been reluctant to accept. In his way of thinking, A La Muerte was untouchable. Mariposa would not forget the challenge to his authority.

"This is not a good day," the drug lord said. "We

have both lost people to this American. Who is he, Candy? You owe me a full explanation."

"Hell, Ramon, ain't much more I know about him than what I already told you, and that's the truth."

They walked to the Hummer and climbed in the back together. Mariposa's bodyguards got in the front, one of them taking the wheel. Candy sank onto the soft leather seat as the heavy vehicle moved off.

"I took a contract for Jessup," Candy explained. "He wants this guy Escobedo put down hard. And he wants it done thorough. Dead and buried."

"Because Escobedo can point a finger at him. Yes, I understand Jessup's concern. No problem there. But I have to ask the question again. This hombre who killed your men and now mine—who is he?"

"We got no background on him so far. No way of telling what outfit he works for."

"He handles himself well."

"Don't remind me. You located him yet?"

Mariposa nodded. "I had people out from late yesterday. They spotted the 4x4 an hour after dawn. He's still moving south, in the same general direction."

"I hope you told your people to stay well back this time. This guy is sharp enough to spot a tail. Like he did already."

"Don't worry, Candy. I put my best people on this. They know what happened to the others, so they will stay invisible." The Mexican flashed a wide smile. "You will have to take my word. We will find your man and allow him to lead us to this Hermano Escobedo."

"That little son of a bitch has caused Jessup a lot of problems."

"I understand, and I will help all I can. Jessup is a good customer and a better friend. He opened the way for A La Muerte to gain access into the United States. I do not forget my friends."

The drive lasted twenty minutes, terminating at the sprawling hacienda Mariposa owned, his home and his business headquarters. The high gates swung open to admit the Hummer, and they followed the curved drive up to the imposing two-story structure. It was not the first time Candy had been here, and as always, he was impressed by the place. Mariposa had lavished money on it, inside and out. Armed guards patrolled the area, watching the house and the grounds. Out back was a wide patio, a swimming pool, tennis courts and tended gardens.

The Hummer parked alongside a number of equally expensive vehicles. Candy walked with Mariposa toward the big house, his bodyguards following close behind. They went inside and crossed the wide hallway, entering a large, open room.

Mariposa gave orders and he and Candy were left alone.

"I won't say I am pleased at what has happened," Mariposa said. He sprawled in a pale leather armchair. "But I am sure neither you nor Jessup are happy, either."

Candy took a seat, spreading his arms across the leather. "What can I say, Ramon. It's a damned embarrassment. Between us, we've lost five men. Escobedo is still on the loose. Hell, none of this makes any of us look good."

Soft footsteps sounded as a white-clad man appeared. He carried a large silver tray holding a coffeepot and mugs. He placed the tray on a low table and vanished as silently as he had appeared.

"Help yourself," Mariposa said.

The hot coffee was rich and had a flavor Candy could appreciate.

"Tell me how this all started," Mariposa said.

Candy explained what Jessup had told him about Escobedo filming two murders on his phone, then vanishing after they'd intercepted his rendezvous with the US Marshals.

"And you believe he crossed the border?" Mariposa asked.

"Yeah. Escobedo is a loner. He doesn't have many friends around Broken Tree. Kind of guy who does his job and stays peaceful. Ain't nowhere he has friends out of town. Doesn't own a car. Seemed more than likely he'd choose to go home."

"That would be my choice. Do we know where he came from?"

"Nope. We're still looking."

"Yet this American who took out your men in Escobedo's apartment appears to have come up with a possible location. Otherwise he would not be traveling across Mexico and having a confrontation with my men."

"What can I say, Ramon? This guy came out of nowhere and just pitched in."

"Is he some kind of cop? Undercover? Maybe a government agent?"

"We can ask him when we catch up."

"Just before he dies," Mariposa said. "We both have scores to settle with this *cabrón*."

He snatched up one of the phones in the room

and began to speak in Spanish. Candy didn't know the language well enough to follow, but he heard the angry tone in Mariposa's voice. When he was finished the Mexican slammed the phone down.

"I wonder at times why I pay these fucking idiots."

"Problems?"

"There is a helicopter sitting out back. It is supposed to be ready to be used at all times. Now they tell me it can't be airborne for at least the rest of the day. It is being serviced and it's disabled while they work on it."

Mariposa vented his anger in an outburst of Spanish, his rage unsettling even to Candy, who knew the man well.

Candy decided not to say anything until Mariposa calmed down. He had heard about the drug lord's propensity to fly into wild rages when things failed to go his way.

Candy refilled his coffee cup and stood quietly by, waiting for his host to regain control. Meanwhile he heard his cell ring, and took it out of his pocket. The caller ID showed it was his man back in Texas.

"This better be good," Candy said into the phone.

"Things not so rosy in Old Mexico?"

"Just tell me, Lorenzo."

"I might have a line on where our runaway is heading."

"I'm listening."

"We know Escobedo is pretty much a loner. And he doesn't own a car. No driver's license. So I figured he might have taken a bus. He buys a ticket and he's gone. I went to the depot here in Broken Tree. Buses run across the border all the time."

"And that means a lot of Mexicans buy tickets."

"Take a breath, Candy. Listen to your buddy Lorenzo. I talked to Jessup's admin guy. You know, Hatton. He runs security for Jessup. Keeps tabs on anyone working the ranch house. Makes 'em all wear those ID tags around their necks. Name, photograph. He ran me off a copy so I could show it around. I took it to the bus depot and it paid off. Spoke to a pretty little gal who recalled our guy. Said he was acting a little nervous when he bought his bus ticket. One way, all the way. To a shit little village called Ascensión. A one-burro spot way out in the Chihuahua boonies."

Candy was silent as he took in what Lorenzo was saying. He weighed the information. It sounded logical, Escobedo losing himself in some backwater Mexican town.

"That good enough?" Lorenzo said. "Makes sense to me."

"Could be right, buddy. You done good. Run some background on this Ascensión. See if there's any connection. Maybe friends. Even family." Candy paused. "Could be that's where our American is heading, looking for Escobedo. Hey, keep me in the loop."

Candy repeated the conversation to Mariposa. The Mexican crossed to a large wall map and traced a line with his finger along the highway that ran from the border deep into Chihuahua. His finger stopped and he jabbed at the map.

"There," he said.

Candy focused on the spot.

Just off the main route, a minor road led into a range of low hills.

And the village of Ascensión.

"Escobedo," Candy said. "You can run, but you damn well can't hide."

RAMON MARIPOSA WAS STILL in a bad mood. With Candy on his heels, he crossed to where his maintenance crew were gathered around the Sikorsky S-76. The repair to the aircraft had been held up due a problem fitting a new engine part. The crew was aware of the cartel boss's anger at the delay. If they had also known Mariposa's temper was mainly fueled by the deaths of the team following the American, they would have worked even harder.

When Candy had asked for help, Mariposa had agreed out of professional courtesy. Seb Jessup was a reliable customer and also provided backup within the USA whenever Mariposa needed it. So it was good for client relations to help the man.

But there was another consideration: his own reputation. Something Ramon Mariposa held dear, because within the drug culture, saving face was paramount. He was the head of A La Muerte, a significant and—up to now—untouchable organization. If word got out that a lone American had invaded his territory it would become open season on his operation. Competitors were always ready to fall on a weaker cartel. Mariposa did not want to find himself in a local war, his territory under siege and his people attacked. He had seen it happen before; wholesale bloodletting could erupt quickly. So this damned American, whoever he was, had to be stopped before his exploits became common knowledge.

Beyond the residential area of his estate stood the

hangar and outbuildings where Mariposa housed his helicopter, and next to it was a concrete landing pad for the aircraft. That was where Mariposa was making his way now, to find out just when the Sikorsky would be ready to fly.

The helicopter repair crew was currently the object of his anger. They all knew it and hastened their attempts to complete the work on the Sikorsky. An explanation existed, but every man understood Mariposa would have no interest in anything they had to say. He saw only that his aircraft was still grounded. He needed it. Now. The delay was their fault—there was no getting around that.

Luis Reynosa, the crew's chief, moved to meet Mariposa. It would not be the first time the man had faced his anger.

"I take the blame," he said directly. "The boys have been working hard to get everything right."

Mariposa stared at him. "This could not have come at a worse time, Luis. Some of our men are already dead. I need to be with my people, but my helicopter is sitting here on the ground…and why?" The drug lord's voice rose to a shout. "Tell. Me. Why!"

"Because I let you down, *Jefe*. I should have worked harder to repair the problem."

For a moment, Mariposa considered hitting Reynosa. His hands were clenched into hard fists at his sides, veins swelling in his neck and face. His anger had him in its grip as he leaned in closer to Reynosa. Then he shrank back, away from the confrontation, and unclenched his fists.

"Get that machine ready, Luis. No more excuses.

If it is not in the air very soon I will hold you responsible. And I will pull the trigger myself."

Reynosa nodded slowly, not saying a word. Sweat beaded across his brow and a dark circle formed around his collar. The frightened man turned to face his crew, simply nodding to them.

The drug lord had given them a final chance. Any more delays and he would make his threat come true.

FOLLOWING IN MARIPOSA'S SHADOW, Candy could understand how the repair crew chief must be feeling. The boss would not go back on his threat. There was no getting away from the fact that Ramon Mariposa was one scary mother.

Mariposa on one side, Seb Jessup the other. Candy was in middle, doing his best to please them both. Definitely between a rock and a hard place.

"Eight million US dollars I paid for that thing," Mariposa said. "Eight million and it can't fly because of a broken part."

As they neared the house he began to shout out orders in rapid Spanish that went over Candy's head after the first few words. His message got across, however, and a number of the cartel shooters gathered their weapons and backup supplies, and piled into a pair of SUVs. The vehicles sped away, raising dust as they hit the side road leading to the highway. Candy watched them go, figuring Mariposa was sending out teams to head for Ascensión. One way or another, the cartel boss was determined to get his people to the area.

Mariposa watched the vehicles until they were out of sight.

"Rohas will cut cross-country, by a different route," he said. "With luck, he may arrive in Ascensión first."

"With luck?"

"Yes. The way he's chosen is extremely difficult. No real trail. Bad terrain, but it could cut off many miles. Rohas believes he can make it." Mariposa shrugged. "He may do it. We have little choice but to take these chances." The drug lord's words were still edged with disappointment that he couldn't respond faster. "If that damn helicopter ever gets off the ground, it will cover the distance to Ascensión in a quarter of the time."

He turned to Candy. "This damned *yanqui* of yours is causing me more problems than I've had in the last six months. Can your people not find out who this asshole is?"

"Ain't for want of trying, Ramon. It's like he just came out of thin air and started all this shit going."

Mariposa said, "He doesn't wear tights and a cape, by any chance?"

"Well, I ain't set eyes on him myself, but he can't be anything more than a man."

Mariposa managed a smile. "Let us hope you are right, my friend, because if he *is* a man, then he can die just like any other."

9

Ascensión, Chihuahua

Mack Bolan drove through the night, stopping only
to top up the 4x4's gas tank and buy a couple cups
of coffee. According to his GPS, he would reach Ascensión by early afternoon.

The drive along the dusty, deserted road left him
with plenty of time to air his thoughts. And upper-
most was something that had begun as a thin irritation
and quickly developed into something more tangible.

The appearance of the armed trio the previous day
meant he had serious competition. Jessup, by whatever method, had worked out that Bolan was on Hermano Escobedo's trail. Add the fact that Jessup had
connections to the local drug cartel and Bolan had
taken out three of its members, and that could spell
trouble. Bolan didn't like having the local drug dealers on the case. They had a better knowledge of the
area than he did.

That shortened the odds.

Made it tougher on Escobedo.

Drug cartels had long arms. They would ask questions in a manner Bolan would never use. Money and violence were the main negotiating tools A La Muerte wielded. If they were unable to get what they wanted by threats, a brutal beating, even torture, might yield better results.

Bolan pushed down on the gas pedal, urging the 4x4 to the maximum. There was also the lingering possibility there might be A La Muerte hands reaching out to local law. It was a sad fact, not to be ignored, that the drug cartels used their vast wealth to buy certain favors. Bolan couldn't justify his suspicions without tangible proof; he was simply going on past experience of the undeniable power the cartels wielded.

Within the next hour, he saw some traffic—a couple dusty trucks and an old station wagon, complete with weathered wood trim. They were all traveling in the opposite direction. He kept a check on the surrounding landscape. There was not a lot to see. The terrain was reasonably flat, semi-arid, dotted with shrubs and the occasional stunted tree. Way off to the west, Bolan could see a sweep of low mountains. It was harsh country.

The satnav display showed the turnoff a half mile ahead. From there it was no more than a couple miles to Ascensión. Bolan slowed the vehicle and watched for the side road. It was unpaved, an uneven, dusty strip that curved up a gentle slope.

He saw the church first, rising above the roofs of the town's other structures. Its slightly crooked bell tower stood white against the sky. As Bolan drove closer, he could see the weathered adobe buildings that made up Ascensión. When the 4x4 rolled onto the main street, the first thing Bolan noticed was the absence of any other vehicles.

He slowed to a crawl, eyeing the few shops. One was a photographer's studio shared with a barbershop. It crossed Bolan's mind it could have been the establishment that had taken the shot of the village that had set him on the road to Ascensión in the first place.

The few people in view watched with curiosity as Bolan pulled up to the church steps. In a place like Ascensión, the church would be the place to ask questions. Bolan made sure his leather jacket was closed over the holstered Beretta as he climbed out of his vehicle.

The weathered doors were open, and he strolled inside. He felt the quiet calm fold around him. Religion did not have much of a place in Bolan's universe. He had seen too much in his life to believe in deities that promised things they could not deliver. Bolan had also seen how people could twist religion and use it as an excuse to wage brutal war against nonbelievers.

"What is it you seek, my son?" someone asked in Spanish

Bolan glanced up and saw a robed figure standing a few feet from him. "My Spanish is a little rusty, Father," he said.

"Then we will speak in English," the priest replied. "I always enjoy an opportunity to practice. There are not many in Ascensión who do speak English."

"Thank you for your tolerance. My name is Matt Cooper."

The man's face creased with pleasure as he extended a hand to draw Bolan farther into the church. "You are welcome, Senor Cooper. I am Father Xavier. I suspect you have not come to seek guidance on the expected harvest of corn this season. Or the yield of sheep or goats."

"My need is not for spiritual information, Father. I'm looking for something more physical."

Bolan followed the priest through the main part of the church and into the private quarters at the far end. They sat on simple wooden chairs, facing each other, and Father Xavier nodded to himself as if reaching a decision.

"I would venture a guess that you are seeking one of my flock who has only recently returned to Ascensión. Yes?"

"You understand me too well, Father."

"Don't assume I have unearthly powers, Senor Cooper. It is not often we receive visitors. Especially those who have traveled all the way from the other side of the border. I see there is no use in pretending I am ignorant as to why you are here."

"I am looking for Hermano Escobedo. I have come to offer him my protection. His life is in danger from men who want him dead. To prevent him from speaking the truth about something he witnessed back in Texas."

"Why would I take it on myself to believe you? A stranger who comes to Ascensión looking for Escobedo. Who tells me he wishes no harm to Hermano. I may only be a simple village priest, but I understand the ways of the world, and you may even be one of the men who wants to kill Hermano. Simply hiding your true intent behind clever words. As you hide your pistol beneath your coat."

Father Xavier stood and crossed to the small stove, his lean hands quick and sure as he poured boiling water in cups to make coffee. He handed one to Bolan.

"Father, I can only tell what I know to be *my* truth. In Texas I found men searching Escobedo's rooms. They were looking for evidence that would point them to the place he had gone. They were not good men and I was forced to deal with them."

"Tell me. Did you kill them?"

Bolan looked the priest in the eyes. "Yes," he said. "And when I drove into Mexico I was forced to kill again. Men belonging to the drug cartel A La Muerte are also looking for Escobedo."

"A La Muerte?" the priest echoed, wringing his hands. "Are you sure?"

"Positive."

"The worst of the worst. They kill without thought. Destroy lives that threaten their vile business. If they come to Ascensión my people will not stand a chance against them."

"The sooner I find Escobedo and take him away, the better for the village, Father. Help me. Has he been here?" Bolan drank the last of his coffee and pushed himself to his feet. "I wish it was otherwise, but he may have put Ascensión in danger by coming here."

Father Xavier extended his hands in a gesture of acceptance. "I cannot allow that to happen," he said.

"What I've told you, Father, *is* the truth. I have to find Escobedo. Get to him before these drug dealers find him. If they do, his life is over and the evidence he has against the men who are after him will be lost."

A series of shouts reached their ears. As they returned to the main area of the church, a white-clad figure ran toward them. The man was speaking so fast Father Xavier had to ask him to repeat himself. Finally he grabbed the man and shook his shoulders, calming him. He fired questions that got him frantic answers.

"It would seem you are right, Senor Cooper. Men in a big utility vehicle are coming toward the village. And they are carrying guns."

"Get him out of here," Bolan said.

The priest urged the panicked man to leave, then followed Bolan out onto the church steps. The soldier spotted the stream of dust being kicked up by the wide tires of a jeep as it headed for the top of the slope leading into Ascensión.

Bolan stripped off his leather jacket, exposing the holstered Beretta. He opened the rear of the 4x4 and took out the Uzi. He had already loaded a fresh magazine following his earlier confrontation with the drug lord's men. He slipped a second magazine under his belt.

"*Por Dios*," Father Xavier whispered. "Has it come to this?"

"Father, you don't face men like these with holy words and a prayer. They would shoot you down before you could make the sign of the cross."

"Unfortunately, my son, you are probably right."

"Get back inside and close the doors." Bolan glanced at the priest. "Do it, Father, now."

He nodded, deferring to Bolan's hard tone of voice and cold expression. The priest turned and hurried inside, closing the timber door behind him.

Bolan remained on the steps, waiting to face the truck and whoever was inside it.

THE TRIP HAD been long and unpleasant. Although the jeep was equipped for traveling over rough terrain, no suspension was going to make such a journey comfortable. The landscape was undulating, the off-road travel primitive.

Rohas, in charge of the open-backed vehicle, found he was having to use the steering wheel as a way of remaining upright as much as guiding the truck toward Ascensión.

The men in the rear were forced to hang on to the steel support bars, and choked from the dust that the wheels threw up. Rohas drove as steadily as he could, taking the vehicle across as much smooth terrain as possible. He stopped a couple times to allow his crew to relax, climbing out from behind the wheel to stretch his own aching body.

"Hey, Rohas, it would be more comfortable to walk," one of his men said.

"You think riding in the cab is easier?"

The man laughed. He took a long swallow of water from his canteen, rinsing out his mouth and spitting.

"Come and taste some of this dust we're swallowing."

Rohas checked their position, pointing at the low hills in the distance.

"Ascensión is over there," he said. "Another few minutes and we should be able to join the road. Morales and his boys will be a couple hours behind us."

"At least they'll have a smooth ride."

Rohas turned to climb back into the driver's seat, ignoring the comment.

He had made an accurate estimation. Within a few minutes he eased the truck off the rough ground and onto the comparatively smooth narrow side road that led directly to Ascensión. With their destination only a few miles ahead the men in the back checked and readied their weapons. They were anticipating some action if they located the American.

Rohas leaned on the gas pedal as the jeep hit the final slope before the village. He thumped his fist on the back of the cab, telling his crew they were almost there.

As they crested the hill, Rohas saw the small community spread out in front of them. The white adobe houses; the church; a dusty 4x4 near the steps.

And a tall figure turning to face them as they rolled toward him.

The man held a squat SMG in his hands, and it was trained on them.

Rohas needed no introduction. He knew he was looking at the man they had come to find.

The American.

The man they had come to kill.

10

Ascensión

Bolan made out one figure in the front of the jeep, and
three more swaying with the motion of the speeding
vehicle in the open back, gripping the roll bar. They
were all armed with AK-74s. The driver spun the
wheel as they pulled up to the church, the shooters in
the rear swiveling around to confront Bolan through
the cloud of dust churned up. He saw the muzzles of
the AK-74s turn in his direction. No negotiations.
Only the sudden threat from the trio of weapons.

The crackle of automatic fire broke the relative
calm of the village.

Streams of 5.45 mm slugs hammered Bolan's vehicle, tearing at the body and wheels, shattering glass.
As he went to ground he caught a glimpse of the 4x4
rocking under the impact of the gunfire. Then one of
the shooters turned his weapon in Bolan's direction.

From destruction to death.

Bolan's death.

The new arrivals had had their fun wrecking Bolan's vehicle. It was their mistake. They should have faced him first

He brought the Uzi around and pulled the trigger. The 9 mm, set on full-auto, threw out a line of slugs, and the shooter's body shuddered under the impact. He fell back across the truck, bloody holes in his torso, and toppled out of sight over the far side.

Bolan held the trigger back and aimed at the next guy, tearing up his abdomen as well, then gave the third man the same treatment. As the bloodied bodies dropped, Bolan rolled, coming up on one knee as he executed a swift magazine change. He worked the cocking slide, loading the first round into the breech, and fired through the side window of the cab as the passenger door started to swing open. Glass blew inward, showering the driver with shards and 9 mm slugs.

Bolan rose to his full height, closing in on the jeep. He blew the front and rear tires and laid more slugs into the engine compartment until smoke began to issue from under the hood and the motor died. Then he raked the cab again, until all movement ceased. Blood was smeared across the inside of the splintered windshield. The silence following the bursts of fire was pronounced.

Bolan moved around the truck, reloading the Uzi again, and checked the road. Nothing in sight. He considered his position in the aftermath of the gunfight. He didn't need to inspect his 4x4 to know the concentrated hits had disabled it. He'd have to find an alternate means of transport, and from what he could see there didn't appear to be any vehicles in the village. If that was the case, Bolan was on foot. It wouldn't be the first time.

He heard a sound behind him, and turned to see Father Xavier emerging from the church. The priest's face betrayed his shock as he came down the steps and stood a few feet from Bolan.

"Will others come?" he asked.

"I can only tell you these people are unlikely to give up their search for Escobedo."

"There is little comfort in knowing that, my son."

Bolan opened the rear door of the 4x4 and reached for his duffel bag. He refreshed the Uzi. He was down to his remaining two magazines. Without a word, he walked to the enemy's vehicle and selected one of the AK-74s from the rear. He found a canvas bag that contained a number of 30-round magazines for the weapon. The cartel clearly maintained a robust supply of ammunition. He slung the canvas bag over his shoulder, checking the Kalashnikov as he walked back to his own vehicle.

"Father, I want this to end for Ascensión. I can do that by locating Hermano Escobedo and leaving the area as quickly as possible ."

Father Xavier held his tongue for a while. He was obviously having a problem with the situation. Bolan understood the priest's dilemma. The moment he had returned to Ascensión, Escobedo had condemned the village to a visit by the men seeking him. Xavier had realized that, accepted it, yet now he was faced with a choice. Did he give up Escobedo so that the American could seek him out and take him away, hopefully freeing Ascensión from the violence of the drug gang? Or did he refuse to betray Escobedo's trust, knowing full well the cartel would send more troops looking for the man?

The priest's choices were difficult, Bolan would give him that.

"If I stay around too long and more A La Muerte men come, we could all end up losing," Bolan said. "It's the last thing I want, and I'm pretty certain you feel the same. When Escobedo was here, you promised to keep his presence secret. Am I right?"

"*Sí*. Hermano felt guilty for coming home. That in heading here he could bring his troubles on the village. I told him that made no difference. He had come home because there was nowhere else he could go. A natural thing to do. Asking my forgiveness was not needed."

"Then give me the chance to move him from the area," Bolan said. "To avoid bringing any more trouble to your village. A La Muerte will come here, and you can tell them the American has gone. That you are not shielding him or Escobedo. Let them come looking for me. If I get a head start, I can locate Escobedo and get him far away." Bolan let his words sink in. "As much as we don't want any of this, it is going to happen. So we need to limit the fallout as much as possible. It is a hard choice, Father Xavier. Hate me all you want for being the one who drew the drug gang here, but don't allow it to cloud your judgment. Protect your village. Your people. Guide me to Escobedo and let me take him back across the border."

Bolan noticed a few of the villagers standing in

the distance, fearful of what had happened, but also curious.

"I was going to arrange for Escobedo to go and stay with a friend," Father Xavier said eventually. "A priest who has a church on the coast near Culiacán. It is even farther from Texas, although I can see now that would hardly have saved him, any more than coming here to Ascensión."

"Father Xavier, there is a way back from this. We're both fighting evil forces in our own ways. Point me to Escobedo. Let me help him. I don't expect your blessing, just your earthly assistance."

Bolan began removing the outer layers of his civilian clothing and pulling on his black combat gear. He donned the harness that carried his weapons and ammunition, and strapped on the backpack holding his personal items. He distributed the magazines for his newly acquired AK-74 around the pouches of his harness. He recognized the need to leave the priest to his decision, to back off for the moment.

"When those men do not report in, the others will come looking for them," Father Xavier said finally.

"And if they do, you will tell them what they want to hear. Tell them where Escobedo is hiding. Don't give them an excuse to hurt you or the village."

"If I tell them, they will come after you and Hermano."

"Yes. I'll be ready for them."

The priest sighed. "And will that require more killing?"

"Father, offer me a solution that does not, and I'll willingly take it on board," Bolan said. "Think about who we are liable to be facing, and tell me the answer."

The priest shook his head. "You will be facing A La Muerte. Drug dealers. Well-known for their lack of humanity, and prone to violence."

Bolan placed his hand on the priest's shoulder. "These people will have heard the word *compromise*, but I can assure you they will never practice it."

"Escobedo's family owned a small farm. They grew crops, had a few goats. Nothing very substantial, and they were always struggling. Which is nothing new for this area. It was the reason Escobedo chose to move to America. He hoped to get work so he could earn some money to send back. There were no other children, his mother died many years ago and he never knew his father, so Escobedo was the only one who could support his maternal grandparents. They were already ailing when he left, and they refused to let Escobedo know about the problems at home while he was gone. If he had learned about their troubles, he would have returned and sacrificed his chances in America. The grandparents were old and have both since passed away. Hermano inherited the farm, though he didn't intend to return, as far as I know. Until recently."

Father Xavier gave Bolan the details he'd need to locate Escobedo's farm. His directions were clear and precise, and the soldier estimated the trek would take him four or five hours on foot.

"Stay here a minute," the priest said, after he'd finished giving the directions. He turned and went inside the church.

Bolan inspected the bullet-riddled 4x4 again. He

wasn't expecting a miracle, just harboring a thin hope the vehicle might be salvageable. Which it wasn't. Checking inside, he saw that his opponents' gunfire had torn apart the dashboard. Instruments were wrecked, wires torn, and now he noticed the strong smell of gasoline. He crouched and peered under the vehicle. The tank had been pierced, gasoline dripping from a number of ragged holes.

"Going to be a trick getting my deposit back," he murmured to himself.

Father Xavier appeared. He was carrying a couple canteens and a small satchel. He handed them to Bolan.

"Water and a little food," he said. "God provides."

Bolan took the offering. "*Gracias*, Father."

"*De nada*." Xavier extended both hands in an encompassing gesture. "Even if you do not truly believe, God *will* watch over you."

Bolan smiled as he took a folded ball cap from his pack and pulled it on. "You're a good man, Father Xavier. I hope your faith in me will not be in vain."

11

Chihuahua

The distant storm clouds moved closer. Bolan was aware of their presence. He figured he had maybe an hour before the storm centered over the area he was traversing. By that time, he would be in the tree-lined hills ahead, where the flat terrain gave way to timber and heavy foliage. The rise in the land was obvious now. Every step took him higher. Ascensión lay two hours behind him already, hidden from sight by the uneven landscape. He could see why Escobedo had chosen this place. It was isolated. But it left him on his own, with no protection. Hermano Escobedo had come to this lonely place to escape, but he was also exposed out here. If his enemies found him, he'd be backed into a corner.

Bolan uncapped one of the canteens and took a swallow of water. He checked the trail behind him, seeing no movement.

He was convinced A La Muerte was still coming. The crew that had showed up in Ascensión would not have been alone. More would be on their way.

He set off again, maintaining a steady pace that covered the ground without tiring him. He could feel the sun through his cap, the material of his shirt. Bolan had no trouble following the thin, almost invisible trail Father Xavier had outlined for him. The priest had most likely walked this way himself on more than one occasion. Bolan admired the man's dedication to his people. His faith in his God kept him going in this lonely place.

Bolan kept moving. He noticed a change in the light and saw that the dark clouds were now overhead. The sunlight faded, and minutes later he felt the first raindrops. They came hard and fast, building to a downpour as he moved into the trees. The vegetation bent under the fierce rain. Bolan pushed his way forward, shoulders hunched. Despite the foliage, he was soon drenched.

He held the AK-74 against his chest. The weapon was locked and loaded. Some instinct told him pursuit was not far behind. He had not seen anything, but countless combat situations had planted the intuitive senses that warned him when danger was close. A La Muerte was not far behind. The storm was unlikely to stop them.

If they came within range, Bolan would.

The ground underfoot quickly became waterlogged. He spotted a couple streams running down the hillside. They had already overflowed their banks, the water white with foam.

Farther Xavier's directions kept Bolan moving

higher. By his calculations, in a couple miles he would break free from the treed slopes and find himself above the wide plain where the Escobedo property was located.

He turned, standing on a section of exposed ground that allowed him to look back the way he had come. A moving object below the tree line caught his eye. Even through the sheet of heavy rain, Bolan could make out the shape of an SUV. It was heading up the slope in his general direction, and he didn't need any more convincing about who was riding in the vehicle.

A La Muerte.

His enemies were on their way.

THERE WERE SIX cartel soldiers in the SUV.

Benito Salazar, riding alongside the driver, had been scanning the way ahead through powerful binoculars. The information they'd got from the priest back in Ascensión had confirmed that the American had been in the village. The holy man had not been able to deny it. There were two disabled vehicles and four fallen cartel men.

Father Xavier had given up his knowledge quite freely, seeming almost too eager to provide it. Of course, there had been the incentive of a knife held against his throat.

Directions in hand, the men had climbed back into the SUV and driven out of Ascensión, leaving the village and the padre intact. Not one of Mariposa's men had felt it necessary to murder a priest. That was a sacrilege none of them wished to be tainted by. Killing came easy to them, but few were willing to risk eternal damnation for the sake of it.

As the SUV crawled up into the hills, Salazar opened the SUV's glass sunroof and stood on the seat, scanning the land ahead with the binoculars. They covered the distance quickly, despite the uneven ground.

Mariposa called them on their sat phone, demanding to know what was happening. When they told him about the dead crew in the first vehicle, his anger became a living thing that threatened to burst through the receiver. The sound of his voice could be heard by all six men in the SUV. The one holding the phone, Espinoza, had no words to respond, so he simply listened.

"You find that *yanqui*. He dies as well as Escobedo. Understand?"

"*Sí, Jefe.*"

"I hold you all responsible. You understand that? This has gone on long enough. A La Muerte cannot let this bastard go free. You follow him. You find him. You destroy him."

The call ended abruptly.

"If we don't find this American I don't believe we should go back," Espinoza said. "He will tear off our cojones with his bare hands."

"Don't say that even as a joke," the driver said.

"What makes you think I was joking?"

"Hey, hombres," Salazar said. "Do you want to know what I think? I think you talk too much. And I have seen the *yanqui* we are looking for."

He slid back down to his seat, activating the button that closed the sunroof. As the panel clicked into place it began to rain. The downpour was heavy, the rain bouncing off the windshield.

"Where?" The driver, Santiago, peered through the glass, which the wipers were struggling to keep clear.

"Directly ahead. He has moved into those trees. Get close. Three of us can follow him. The rest of you line up along the edge of the trees and watch in case he comes out again."

They each checked their weapons and put on the comsets they carried, making certain they were all on the same channel.

"Remember what Mariposa said," Espinoza warned. "I have no intention of losing my cojones, so let us track this damned American and kill him. Then we go on and find Escobedo."

12

The cartel crew was close. Too close. Bolan didn't intend to move on with them at his heels. If he simply pushed ahead, he might unwittingly lead them to their target. Once he reached Escobedo, he knew they might face more opponents. But Bolan wanted to give himself—and Escobedo—a little more time to prepare for that eventuality.

Bolan watched six fully armed figures climb out of the SUV as it reached the tree line. They were no more dressed for the weather than he was. He stayed put as they grouped together, discussing tactics. In the end, three of them began to trudge through the downpour into the woods. The remaining trio spread out to survey the area.

Bolan pushed his way through the foliage.

Three to deal with first.

Then the ones staying out of the trees.

Bolan was thinking about the SUV. If he could get

his hands on that it would make the rest of his trek to Escobedo's hideout much easier.

The trio separated as soon as they were among the trees. They moved about twenty-five feet apart, then began to walk forward.

Bolan pinpointed each man's line of travel, knowing he might lose them in the dense foliage. But he was going to take the fight to them, and the fact that they had separated would make his task easier.

The guy closest to Bolan's position was coming quickly, with little caution. He was too confident, and it was that attitude that brought him nearer to Bolan than he should have been. Cartel soldiers were used to facing ordinary citizens and using threatening behavior. They had limited tactical experience. The Executioner was about to offer them the real thing.

The man pushed through tangled branches and shrubs, and Bolan shrank back as he approached. He came across a fallen tree, the trunk massive and overgrown with vines and other plants that had sprouted along its gnarled length. Bolan crouched behind it and laid the Uzi and the AK-74 on the ground, unsheathing his Tanto knife. He picked up a low murmur, and the pattern of the guy's speech told Bolan he was speaking into a comset. He was telling his partners he was sure he had their quarry located. That the *yanqui* was close by and he would soon find him and make his kill.

Bolan would have agreed to that. The man *was* near. Very near. He just had the scenario wrong. It would be Bolan finding *him*.

The clink of metal on metal sounded as the cartel soldier took another step closer, his equipment giving him away. He was muttering to himself as he edged around the twisted roots of the tree and then on along its length. He stepped into Bolan's field of vision, and when he tilted his weapon, Bolan caught a dull gleam of light as it rippled along the barrel. That gave him his target and he made use of it.

In one swift motion, the Executioner sprang from his hiding spot, his left hand driving forward to grasp the guy's throat, his right striking hard at the mid-section of the exposed torso. The Tanto's cold blade sliced through clothing and sank in up to the hilt. He felt the man shudder as he slid the penetrating blade left to right to extend the wound. A harsh groan burst from the Mexican's lips. Bolan slid his left hand around the back of the guy's neck, yanking him forward, pulling his body in closer to the cutting blade. He felt warm blood oozing from the stab site. Bolan pushed the weakening man against the log, leaning on him hard, feeling the tremors that followed the damage done by the knife. The guy let out a long, ragged sigh as he began to slip to the ground. Bolan kept up the pressure until all movement and sound ceased. Then he pulled out the knife, cleaned the steel blade against the man's shirt and sheathed it.

He could hear faint noises coming from the headset the man was wearing. Bolan slipped the device from the body, held it close and listened to the transmission. He identified two voices. One ordered the other to silence, then spoke in swift Spanish. "Enrico, what is going on? Talk to me. Where are you?"

"I found him," Bolan said, keeping his voice low. "You want to come and see?"

There was a brief silence.

"You are not Enrico…who are you?"

"The one you cannot find. The one who is going to send you to hell."

A violent shout burst through the comset. Bolan retrieved his weapons, suspending the Uzi by its strap around his neck. He carried the AK-74 in his hands, ready for use, and moved away from the cover of the fallen tree. The cartel members knew he was around and capable of facing whatever they had ready for him. One man down and two still in the vicinity. He listened to the comset, picking out the sound of their movements and the whispered conversation between them.

The heavy downpour would work to his advantage. Anything that would distract his enemies, make them function less as a unit, would allow him to move around with more ease. Flexibility, the ability to slip in and out quickly, these were Bolan's aces. And he would use them well. If he worked it right he could break down their numbers, leave them wondering where the next hit might come from.

Crouching in the shadows, he focused his attention on the comset chatter as the cartel soldiers assessed their next move.

Bolan checked out the AK-74, set the fire rate to single shot. The Kalashnikov was familiar to him and he knew its capabilities; it had a decent range and accuracy. The assault rifle would serve him well as an intermediate sniper weapon.

He focused on peripheral sound, tuning in to the noise the Mexicans made as they moved through the bushes, searching for him. They were not the quietest pair. They brushed against leaves, stepped on twigs and disrupted stones and dirt. Small sounds, but to Bolan they indicated the whereabouts of his quarry.

One man cursed into the comset. Things were not going the way they wanted. These narco warriors expected matters to fall easily into their hands, and when that didn't happen, they allowed their impatience to show. Bolan didn't mind that. If they became unsettled, their concentration would slip. Which would give him a fraction of an advantage.

He turned slightly as he heard someone stumble in the undergrowth off to his right. Bolan leaned forward, squinting in the gray light filtering through the dripping canopy.

Nothing at first. Bolan stayed still. If the guy was close by he would show himself eventually…

And he did.

The bright color of his shirt gave him away. Even in the gloomy light, it stood out. Bolan shouldered the AK and trained the barrel on the figure, raising the muzzle so it pointed at the target's head. The cartel soldier carried a similar model automatic rifle to the one Bolan was holding.

The man's head began to turn toward Bolan as if he had picked up a visual himself.

The Executioner didn't hesitate.

He held the target for a split second longer, then pulled back on the trigger. The AK-74 cracked sharply. The 5.45 slug covered the distance in a breath of time and the guy jerked sideways as it struck the side of his skull, coring through and emerging in a burst of red. Bolan saw the guy fall, all control gone.

The sound carried through the comset like an echo,

followed by a stream of Spanish. A man asking where his partner was.

Now Bolan heard footsteps heading in his direction. He burrowed deeper into the greenery. It wouldn't conceal him at close range, but he hoped he was hidden enough to surprise the approaching enemy.

The guy stepped into a clearing about thirty feet away. He was wearing baggy pants and a sleeveless jerkin over a light shirt. He was also carrying an AK-74, holding it at his side as he glanced around. Water streamed down his face. As he pivoted slightly, Bolan saw he was wearing a holstered automatic pistol on his right hip.

Bolan heard the comset crackle.

He picked up the harsh Spanish as the guy spoke.

"Hey, gringo, I know you can hear me. I just want to let you know I am going to kill you soon. No fooling. You are a dead man. When I have killed you, I will take your fucking head to show my *jefe*…"

The final word that left his mouth was followed by the crack of the shot from Bolan's AK. He put a slug into the guy's head above his left eye. The shot was clean. It traversed the target's skull and blew out the rear, taking bone and brains with it. Blood sprayed from the wound and the guy dropped without a sound.

The moment he'd fired, Bolan withdrew into the deeper foliage, pulling the assault rifle into cover with him. Then he crouched in the shadows, watching and listening for the surviving cartel soldiers on the edge of the forest.

Bolan could hear someone breathing over the comset. The man's air came in short, sharp bursts as he took in what had just happened.

And that he himself was being tracked by the unseen American A La Muerte had come to kill.

Bolan worked his way back to where he'd spotted the SUV. Rain sluiced down through the leaves, but he was already soaked. He could feel it dripping onto his sodden ball cap. He had pulled the AK-74 close to his body so it wouldn't snag on the tangled undergrowth when he moved. He'd cut their team in half, and the remaining soldiers on the scene would be assessing their own position, listening for him to make a sound that would betray his presence. That was fine with him. He had played this game many times. He was comfortable waiting it out, banking on the other guys not being as patient.

The rain began to ease off as the storm moved on, away to the east. The forest became quieter. Bolan held his ground, making no moves that might give him away. He watched the surrounding area intently for any sign of the opposition.

When it came, he might have missed it if he'd blinked.

A tiny disturbance in the branches to his left, maybe twenty feet away. It lasted no more than a second, but it told Bolan someone was close by. He remained motionless, let the other guy initiate action.

The man stepped out of the tangle of tree limbs, half crouching as he moved. He swiveled his head from side to side, surveying the area. He was a big man. Broad across the shoulders and with a heavy torso. Despite his bulk, he was light on his feet.

He stopped suddenly, head coming forward as if he had picked up on something.

Bolan chose his moment. He brought the AK up to his shoulder, drawing a bead on the man's forehead.

The A La Muerte member was staring directly at him now, lifting his own weapon. Bolan's finger was on the trigger, but the Mexican fired first, unwilling to take that extra second to fully engage his target. His shot went wide, ripping at dirt to Bolan's left, shredding leaves. The man fired again, hastily, on full-auto, peppering the tree trunks and forest floor.

Bolan held his position, staying in his crouch. In the microsecond it took the guy to let loose another round, Bolan took aim and fired a single slug, hitting his enemy directly between the eyes. He punched out two more shots and the back of the man's skull exploded from the combined force of the three bullets. He toppled like a felled oak, body rigid, and hit the ground hard.

Two left.

Bolan heard raised voices and heavy breathing through the comset as the cartel soldiers hurried to find their fallen compatriot.

Bolan stayed put for a time, just listening. Finally, satisfied that neither man was nearby, he eased out of concealment far enough to help himself to the extra magazines the guy he'd just shot had been carrying, adding to his own ammunition supply.

As the storm retreated, the temperature began to rise. Bolan's skin dried quickly, then began to gleam with sweat. Through the upper canopy, he saw the sky lighten as the clouds drifted away.

He did a slow scan of the area ahead of him, toward the open terrain where he could make out the shape of the cartel's SUV. That vehicle would give him a huge advantage. He'd be able to cover the rest of the distance to Escobedo's hideout in far less time than it would take him to walk, and he'd get a head start on any additional cartel troops.

But his first priority was taking down the remaining pair.

The comset had fallen silent. Mariposa's men had obviously decided they'd been giving away too much information. Discretion replaced their earlier bravado.

Bolan had to eliminate them as quickly as possible. There could already be others on their way. And each time he took down an A La Muerte member he was twisting the knife. Mariposa's pride was taking a beating and he was not going to accept the fact lightly.

Despite his sense of urgency, Bolan kept still, knowing that patience paid off in this kind of situation. Being a sniper required a certain detachment of mind and body; the stillness that would not betray his presence to the enemy; the keen vision and hearing that would detect the slightest indication of his target's presence. When that moment came, the sniper had to be ready to recognize the sign and react to it. Move too soon and the target might be alerted and slip away. Too late and the tables might easily be reversed, the hunter becoming the hunted.

Bolan had what it took, both physically and mentally, to wait out his prey.

And long minutes later, he saw his chance.

His ears picked up on the stealthy tread of a man off to his right. Bolan shifted imperceptibly toward the sound just as the man broke out of a dense tangle of dripping foliage into a shaft of sunlight. The Mexican was edging forward, his face glistening with sweat. He paused, glancing around, apparently unsure which way to go next.

Bolan's AK-74 was already at his shoulder. His finger rested lightly on the trigger as the cartel soldier came into focus. Bolan held his breath and kept his aim steady, aware that the target might move again and break the shot. The Executioner squeezed the trigger, feeling the cold steel against his flesh. The weapon exploded loudly in the stillness of the forest. Birds erupted from the trees, wings flapping in panic as they rose.

The Mexican's head snapped back as the bullet slammed into his forehead. He went down, a mist of blood fanning out from his shattered skull.

A sustained burst of automatic fire erupted from farther to Bolan's right. He flattened himself on the ground as the shots tore up the area around him. The fire ceased abruptly—likely an empty magazine— and Bolan took the brief respite to break position while the shooter reloaded.

When he moved, the enemy moved, too. He stepped out of cover, left hand snapping in the fresh magazine. The guy was fast with his reload, the barrel rising even as he completed the mag insertion. But his action, smooth as it was, lagged behind his opponent's response. Bolan fired his own AK before his opponent had a finger on the trigger. This time, The Executioner couldn't afford to wait for the perfect shot. He aimed directly at the target and punched out a rapid quartet of 5.45 slugs, which burrowed into the Mexican's chest. The force tossed the guy back and off his feet. He landed hard on the muddy ground, weapon flying out of his fingers.

For now, the odds were back in Bolan's favor. One-nothing.

13

Mariposa led the way out to where the helicopter was warming up. Candy followed, relieved that *something* was happening. Despite the comfort of Mariposa's home, Candy had found it hard to relax. Up to this point, nothing had been going right. Candy didn't enjoy failure and that was what this exercise was proving to be.

He had spoken to Jessup, bringing him up to date. Jessup had been close to losing it when Candy told him the bad news about Mariposa's fallen men.

"Nothing I can do, Seb," Candy had said. "Soon as that whirlybird's warmed up we're goin' after Escobedo and that cop—or whatever he is."

"What about the second crew Ramon sent out?"

"Mariposa's people keep trying, but they can't get through."

"This is going from shit to hell in a handbasket," Jessup yelled. "Hell, Candy, what am I payin' you for?"

"Ain't the way I was expecting it to go, Seb. I hold up my hands. This came at me blind. But the game ain't over yet."

"Just think on it, Candy. If we don't hit a home run by the last quarter, this game ends with me screwed and in a cell. I won't take kindly to that. You hear what I'm saying?"

"I hear, Seb. Loud and clear."

"So get 'er done, boy."

Jessup hung up, and Candy stared at the silent cell phone. Jessup's words left him with a moment of unease. The man had a reputation for never forgiving or forgetting failure. And Seb Jessup always made good on his threats—explicit or implied.

Son of a bitch, Candy thought, that old boy will have my skin for a book cover if I don't deliver.

"Hey, Candy, you ready to go?"

He snapped back to the moment, aware that Mariposa was watching him closely.

"Yeah, ready," he said.

"Everything okay with Seb?"

Candy forced a grin. "Nothing to worry about," he said. He didn't even fool himself.

He followed Mariposa across to where the Sikorsky sat idling, the spinning rotors sucking up dust. Six of Mariposa's crew members were already seated in the rear of the cabin. Every man was fully armed. Mariposa took the seat beside the pilot and Candy climbed in behind them. They each donned their headsets as the helicopter took off.

"Should take us a couple of hours to reach Ascensión," Mariposa said.

"It's going to be night by then," Candy pointed out.

Mariposa laughed. "Hey, amigo, you afraid of the dark?"

"No. I just like to be able to see who might be shooting at me."

"Day or night, my friend, they say you never see the one that gets you."

The chopper rose with the beat of the rotors before making a sharp turn and speeding over the barren landscape. Candy pressed his spine against the seat. He kept it to himself, but in truth he didn't like helicopters. He could face a man under gunfire, take out an adversary with a knife in his hand, but put him in one of these spinning tops and Candy was as close to panicking as he was ever likely to be. But here he was, fulfilling the terms of his contract with Jessup. Phobia or not, Candy would see it through—he smiled at his next thought—even if it killed him.

Mariposa spent a good chunk of the flight on his sat phone, dealing with A La Muerte business. Nothing would come between him and his operation. The man was a Mexican version of Seb Jessup. Business came above anything else. Candy couldn't fault them for their dedication.

In the rear of the chopper, Mariposa's armed crew sat quietly. Some dozed; others simply checked and rechecked their weapons.

Through the side window, Candy could see the landscape flashing by. Open, mostly flat terrain. Almost uniformly dun colored, with occasional islands of greenery. It was dry, dusty country that reminded Candy of the Texas landscape. It could be harsh. Unforgiving.

Candy's headphones clicked and he heard Mariposa's voice.

"You okay, hombre?"

"Yeah."

"You do not enjoy helicopters?"

"Not my favorite method of transport, if I have to be honest."

"You're safe here. Rico is a good pilot. Did you see how well he got us into the air?"

"Getting up here isn't worrying me. It's staying there I have the problem with."

Rain pattered against the helicopter, making a low drumming noise. After a minute, the pilot activated the wipers and made some adjustments to the flight pattern.

"We okay?" Candy asked.

Rico nodded. "I'll fly around the storm. It's moving away from us anyhow. We're just catching the tail end."

"Tail end? That's okay, then," Candy said, which drew a chuckle from Mariposa.

Candy tried to relax, even closed his eyes. Nothing worked.

Rico kept the helicopter on course, flying with a sure hand. After an hour, the rain let up. "See, we're out of the storm now," he announced. "They come and go. When they arrive, it can be very fierce, but they usually blow over quickly."

Candy couldn't raise a cheer at the news. He was thinking about the American. The guy was proving to be a resourceful mother. A pain in the ass for sure, but he was staying ahead at the moment. The more he thought about the man, the more Candy had to admire his ability to stay on his game.

He was a loner, which would be unusual if he was a lawman. They preferred to work in teams. Still, there had to be someone he reported back to. A person he could update on his progress. These guys didn't work in a vacuum. Along the way, he would communicate with a superior. The man, or department, that controlled him. The more Candy thought about it, the more frustrated he became.

Who the hell *was* this guy?

It was early evening when the helicopter swung in over Ascensión. In the glare of the chopper's lights they were able to make out the scattered buildings, including a church. And the pair of vehicles parked on the deserted street.

"So where are your boys?" Candy asked. "No welcome for *El Jefe*?"

"Put us down, Rico," Mariposa said.

The moment they were on the ground, the pilot cut the engine.

Mariposa was the first out, followed by Candy and the crew. Their weapons were drawn as they moved along the open street. Rico powered the helicopter's lights so they focused in on the deserted vehicles. Once they got close enough, Candy saw how badly damaged both were. Shredded tires. Shattered windows. And the bullet holes. The smell of gasoline lingered over the scene.

But no bodies were visible.

Mariposa appeared to be at a loss. "Where are they?" he said. "Where are my men?"

A figure in a simple brown robe emerged onto the

church steps. "If you are seeking your people, they are inside here."

Mariposa confronted the priest. "In the church?"

He nodded. "It was the least I could do for them. Their profession aside, they are still God's children."

Mariposa glanced at Candy, who gave a slight shrug. The meaning was not lost on either of them.

"May I see them, Father…?"

"Xavier. Of course."

Father Xavier stepped aside as Mariposa moved up the steps and through the door.

"There was a second vehicle?" Candy asked.

The priest nodded. "Yes. It came many hours ago. I was questioned by the men and then they drove on."

"They were following the American?"

"Yes."

"He went on foot?"

"There was much gunfire. His vehicle was also disabled, so the American, Cooper, continued without one."

"Cooper?"

"Yes, he called himself Matt Cooper."

"He came looking for Hermano Escobedo? And I'm guessing you offered him directions?"

"It would be foolish of me to deny it after all that has happened."

"Father, it would be foolish for you *not* to offer us those same directions."

"He told me to give them to you. As I did to the other people who came."

"Believing it was better than dying?"

"Despite the certainty we will all die one day, I

saw the wisdom in giving away that information. Your friends who followed had persuasive powers."

Candy smiled. "Father, you play poker? Well, you sure as hell should, 'cause you know just how to work the cards."

Mariposa exited the church and put a hand on the priest's shoulder. "Father, I thank you for what you did for my men. To see them all laid out, washed and tidied up… It was a kindness I will long remember."

"You are welcome, my son. Inside God's house a man's sins can be put aside at the moment of his death."

"I would offer you money for the burials," Mariposa said. "But I can see it would not be welcome. How I earn it cannot be justified in your eyes."

"A debatable point," Father Xavier said. "One we could no doubt discuss if the need arose."

"The padre was just about to give me directions," Candy interjected.

"True?" Mariposa looked to the priest.

"The American advised me to pass along the information. He seemed eager to meet you all."

"I hope you follow his advice," the drug lord said. "After all that has happened here, it would be regrettable if more killing was to follow in your village."

Mariposa spoke quietly, without any threat in his voice, but the underlying suggestion was hard to avoid.

The priest smiled deferentially and offered the same directions he had already given out.

"We will leave you in peace, Father," Mariposa said when he'd finished. "Our business is elsewhere."

"I will bury your men and accord them the last

rites. I would say to you 'Go with God,' but I feel that would be inappropriate."

Mariposa held the priest's stare. A faint smile played at the corners of the *jefe*'s mouth, then he turned on his heel and waved his men back toward the helicopter.

"A close moment, Father," Candy said quietly.

"God was on my side," Xavier said.

"With Mariposa, I wouldn't have liked to bet on the difference," Candy commented, before heading back to the Sikorsky.

14

It was a late-model Cadillac Escalade. A black, four-wheel-drive monster with all the trimmings. When Bolan checked out the SUV, he found it was fitted with every add-on in the book. He had taken his time approaching the vehicle in case it wasn't as empty as it appeared. When he reached it, he found that it posed no threat. He set most of his equipment on one of the back seats, keeping his Beretta in hand as he inspected the luxurious interior, which included an extra fuel tank.

A La Muerte knew how to look after itself.

Bolan eased behind the wheel and hit the start button. The powerful V-8 engine purred to life. He inspected the trees in front of him. There was no chance he could cut through the dense forest, so he'd have to circle around the stand of timber until he was able to rejoin his original path. It would take up valuable time, but was still faster than moving on foot.

The heavy SUV handled easily, responding

quickly to his touch. He drove at a steady speed over the uneven ground. The day had cleared and he could see the pale outline of low mountain peaks far ahead.

Bolan figured he had a couple hours before it got dark. He was in unknown country, and attempting to drive through the night was not a smart idea. He had no way of knowing what kind of terrain lay beyond this small forest, and as much as he needed to reach Hermano Escobedo, it wouldn't do either of them any favors if he ran into trouble before he got there.

When the sun had set and it became clear that the moonlight wasn't going to be much help, Bolan maneuvered the SUV into a shadowy curve in the hillside and cut the motor. He would wait out the night here, then move on at first light. He opened the food bag Father Xavier had given him, and pulled out a hunk of bread and some goat cheese. Bolan ate gratefully and drank from the one of the canteens. Then he settled down to rest. As always, he slept lightly, senses attuned for any suspicious sounds.

Before he allowed himself to sleep, he turned his thoughts to Hermano Escobedo, the reason he was here in the wilds of Mexico.

Bolan wondered how the man was doing, hiding away in his own country. A lone individual with the weight of Jessup's organization ready to crush him, and now the added threat from the cartel. Bolan had yet to meet Escobedo, but knew he must be terrified, unable to trust anyone, isolated and directionless. His position was not enviable.

Bolan intended to change that. At dawn, he would make his final push to reach and extract Escobedo. He had already clashed with A La Muerte soldiers.

It didn't take a great stretch of imagination to realize his previous encounters wouldn't be his last. Jessup and Mariposa were not going to let the matter rest. Sooner or later, Bolan was going need his cleansing firepower to clear the way. This knowledge didn't deter him in the least. He would face what came and deal with it in the moment.

He'd never thought of himself as indestructible; a bullet in the right place could end his life as easily as anyone else's. Dangerous as it was, he'd chosen this path because he'd seen how true evil could flourish, given the right conditions. His ongoing battle, his Everlasting War, was his attempt to redress the balance. Bolan understood he would never win his fight overall, but even the slightest of victories mattered. He could not ask for more. It motivated him to move on and confront the next challenge.

As THE SKY BEGAN to lighten, Bolan woke and climbed out of the SUV. He took a few swallows from the canteen and glanced around. Seeing nothing out of the ordinary, he made a cursory check of the SUV's tires in case they'd been damaged on the rough terrain he'd driven over the previous day.

Behind the wheel, Bolan started the engine and maneuvered the SUV out of its hiding place. He worked out his position and set himself back on course.

The big SUV took to the slopes easily. Bolan picked up the faint traces of a trail and drove at a steady pace, alert to anything that might suggest others were closing in on Hermano Escobedo, as well. Bolan wasn't about to underestimate the opposition.

Midmorning, he saw his first signs of life—a few goats roaming loose on the hills ahead of him. He recalled Father Xavier mentioning there were several at the Escobedo farm.

Bolan braked and pulled out the binoculars the A La Muerte men had left in the SUV. The incline he was on ran down to a flat stretch of ground that held a small house and some outbuildings. Father Xavier had described it perfectly, even down to the small well in the yard. Movement caught Bolan's attention; a thin drift of smoke was coming from the chimney. He spent some time studying the farm and the surrounding area. He saw nothing to suggest anyone besides Escobedo was here.

He drove down the slope to the house, and when he cut the motor, realized how quiet the place was. Bolan picked up his Uzi and silently exited the vehicle.

The whole farm showed a lack of attention. Fence rails down, equipment scattered around, grass and weeds sprouting up everywhere. A few chickens wandered back and forth.

Bolan was not convinced he was on his own. He walked around the SUV, then stood with his back to the vehicle as he inspected the house.

"Hermano Escobedo, step out so I can see you. I'm here to take you to safety. Back to the US, so you can present your evidence against Seb Jessup. My name is Matt Cooper." He paused, waiting for any indication of Escobedo's presence. Nothing.

"I understand your position," Bolan continued. "If I was in your shoes, I'd feel the same. I've come on behalf of the Justice Department. We need to get out of here fast, because Jessup's allies are on their way.

Members of the A La Muerte cartel. Ramon Mariposa's men. Your good friend Father Xavier helped me locate you…"

Bolan waited. Still nothing.

Why would Escobedo believe him?

Who could the poor man trust?

"Escobedo—Hermano—if I was with Jessup or Mariposa I would not be on my own. Those people are only strong when they work in groups. None of them have the courage to face anyone on their own."

Bolan let it end there. He could plead his case for only so long. It was up to Escobedo to make his own decision. If he was inside the house, he had to choose. Either way, the man was in no position to run, now that his hiding place had been discovered.

Bolan fixed his attention on the adobe-and-timber structure. He could understand Escobedo's reluctance to show himself. Doubt would be weighing heavily on the man.

The front door creaked opened slowly, revealing a shadowed figure standing inside. Bolan recognized the face from the photograph he had seen at Stony Man.

Hermano Escobedo.

As the Mexican advanced a few feet, Bolan saw that he was unshaved, his face a little thinner than in his photo. He simply stood and stared at the American.

"So how do you intend to save me?" he asked. "If that is truly what you're here for."

"By getting us both away from this place. Mariposa will send his people to look for you. I left a crew dead in Ascensión. Others back along the road. Mariposa will send more."

Escobedo moved out of the doorway, his eyes scanning the area restlessly. "You could be working for Jessup," he said. "Simply drawing me into the open so you can kill me."

"If that was the case, I would have already shot you."

"Unless you are playing with me. Letting me believe you bring help, before I die."

"Hermano, I am not deceiving you. I *have* come to help."

"Is this true? That you killed men who were hunting me?"

"Yes. I had no choice. They were ready to shoot me down if I hadn't done it to them first."

All the time Escobedo listened to Bolan, he never stopped looking around suspiciously. It was obvious he wanted to believe his words, but was finding it difficult. Bolan spotted the heavy knife the fugitive gripped in his right hand. It had been hidden by the leg of his pants, but became exposed when he moved forward.

"Father Xavier thinks a great deal of you. He told me about this place. How it belonged to your grandparents until they died. It must have been hard for you to come back."

"What choice did I have? Jessup's men made it impossible for me to stay in Broken Tree. They murdered the two policemen sent to protect me. They would have killed me then, too. Who else could I trust after that? I had to make a choice. So I came back here to hide, and to decide what I'd do next."

"And what is it you want to do?"

"I want to see Seb Jessup pay for what he did. For murdering those young people. And for other crimes he's likely guilty of."

"Then let's do that, Hermano. Go back to the US and testify. Let me make sure you can point your finger at Jessup and have him put away."

"He will do everything he can to prevent that."

"People don't always get what they want."

Escobedo was quiet for a moment, considering. "Can we do this? Against all these people?"

"We can give it a damn good try." Bolan slapped a hand against the side of the vehicle. "And our enemies have supplied us with the transport to do it."

"Let me collect my things," Escobedo said.

When he came back outside, he had a backpack over his shoulder.

"Let's go," Bolan said, sliding into the driver's seat.

Escobedo stared out the window as they left the farm behind. "This is the second time I have walked away from my home," he said. "When I left before, I was going to find a new life in America."

"We can still make that happen, Hermano. If you're willing to take a stand against Jessup, anything is possible."

"I imagine even Father Xavier would find a miracle like that hard to accept."

"Then we need to convince him."

15

The helicopter dropped quickly, swinging in over the farm buildings, dust swirling in gritty clouds. Under Rico's sure hand, the aircraft held in a steady hover.

"You think he's in there?" Candy asked.

Mariposa snapped out orders. Two of his crew checked their weapons and moved to the side hatch. They dropped ropes and went down hand over hand, letting go for the last few feet. The instant they hit the ground, they converged on the house. They kicked the door down and went inside. They emerged quickly and Candy saw one of them shake his head.

"Son of a bitch is gone," Candy said.

"That will be your American," Mariposa growled. "Your Matt Cooper. I'm going to enjoy putting a bullet in that hombre."

Rico set the chopper down some distance from the house. Mariposa climbed out, Candy close behind. They met up with the men already on the ground.

"Someone has been living in the place for a while," one of them said. "Ashes in the fire are still warm."

Another soldier waved a hand to the north of the property. "Tracks," he said. "Wide tires, like the ones on our missing SUV. I think the *yanqui* has been here and taken Escobedo away with him."

"Cooper will make a run for the border," Candy said.

"Then let's make sure he doesn't make it," Mariposa retorted. "There is nothing but empty country between here and the US. We'll spot him now we know which way he'll be going. *Vámonos.*"

They all returned to the helicopter. Rico boosted the power and the aircraft rose from the Escobedo farm. It gained height, then angled to the north.

"That son of a bitch knows how to turn a situation to his advantage," Candy said. "Takes down your guys and commandeers their vehicle."

"A good soldier makes the most of what he can salvage." Mariposa shrugged. "Losses or gains, he picks the best from every battle."

The guy will want to pin a medal on Cooper next, Candy thought.

He slumped in his seat, considering how Jessup would respond to the latest developments. He certainly wouldn't be as casual as Mariposa. Jessup would be ready to tear out Cooper's insides and feed them back to him raw. What he would do with Escobedo didn't even bear thinking about.

They'd been flying only a few minutes when Rico pointed out movement below. It was a vehicle.

"See, I knew we would find them," Mariposa said.

"Go down. Get close to them. *Muchachos*, have your weapons ready."

Rico maneuvered the helicopter, dropping altitude and taking the aircraft in a long, swooping trajectory that brought it in line with the SUV. On his first pass, he flew low over the vehicle, causing it to swerve. The tires threw up clouds of dust.

"Again," Mariposa said. "I want him to see he cannot avoid us."

THE CHOPPER BUZZED the SUV twice, causing the vehicle to sway in the backdraft. Bolan didn't see any law enforcement insignia on the bird, and he didn't need much else to tell him this was an A La Muerte attack. Maybe even Mariposa himself.

Bolan figured the pilot was doing his best to unnerve him. Maybe even cause him to crash. If the guy became ambitious, he might even try to nudge the SUV. The only point in Bolan's favor was that there had been no gunfire. Yet.

He accelerated, pulling ahead of the aircraft, then slammed on the brake and came to a sudden stop. The chopper overflew the SUV, and in the short time it took to double back, Bolan ordered Escobedo out of the vehicle.

He had spotted a clump of boulders about fifty yards away.

"Get to those rocks," he shouted. "No time for explanations, Hermano. Just do it. Now. Stay under cover until I tell you different."

Escobedo turned and sprinted away, disappearing among the boulders as the chopper came overhead once more.

Bolan stepped out of the vehicle, shouldering the AK-74. No bullets had been fired from the aircraft, but he wasn't about to let A La Muerte have the first shot.

16

Cooper started firing as soon as the low-flying chopper made its next pass. His first shots were off target, but the follow-up rounds found their mark, punching holes through the aluminum fuselage and forcing Rico to veer away from his position.

As the helicopter turned aside, Candy watched the man take a moment to steady his rifle, then he fired again, even as Rico fought to gain height.

The American scored another hit, this time placing a shot through one of the side windows.

The Plexiglas exploded, showering the crew with splinters. The slug hit one of Mariposa's men in the neck, tearing a ragged hole and severing his carotid artery. Blood began to spurt from the ugly wound. The guy clasped a hand to his throat, then keeled over, blood flowing in copious amounts as his heart pumped it from his body.

Mariposa began to curse, loudly. In the rear of the cabin, the other men were all calling out advice to one another, but they were killers, not medics, and none of them knew what to do. In truth, Candy realized, the guy who had taken the hit was a dead man from the moment the slug made contact.

Sure enough, the flow of blood began to slow as the man's heart failed. Finally, his head lolled to the side and his eyes glazed over.

"Circle back," Mariposa screamed at Rico. "There's no way that bastard is getting away now."

The pilot shook his head. "We can't get too close. He's too good a shot."

"Then set down out of range and we go in on foot. I will not play games any longer. We land and we go after him."

Candy fingered his borrowed AK-74. He was no coward. He had stalked and killed his share. But there was something about Cooper that worried him. Something that—and he hated himself for even thinking it—scared him. He couldn't figure out what it was. The guy had the ability to overcome anything that stood in his path. He clearly had combat experience that enabled him to take on bigger odds and walk away. Candy only had to think back to the Jessup men he had taken down in Broken Tree. Then the list of A La Muerte shooters here in Mexico. The nervy son of a bitch just kept coming, regardless.

Candy had to admire Cooper's skill. The way he kept knocking back the opposition. All things considered, maybe a man was right to be nervous going up against him. Cooper wasn't invincible, but he was doing a damn good job convincing everyone he was.

Rico lowered the chopper, touching down with barely a bump. As the aircraft settled he cut the power, the rotors making a whooshing sound as they began to slow. Mariposa's crew disembarked, taking the dead guy with them. They laid his bloody corpse on the ground, then stripped him of weapons and spare magazines, distributing them among themselves.

"Let's move," Mariposa ordered. "Find them. Kill them both."

His soldiers moved off. Mariposa and Candy watched them go, then fell in at the rear.

"Jesus," Candy muttered. "My momma was right when she told me never to leave Texas."

BOLAN SAW THE helicopter move away, clearing the area. It started to descend, then slipped out of sight behind some low hills. He waited long enough to confirm it wasn't veering back toward them, then went to find Escobedo among the boulders.

"What's happening?" the Mexican asked.

Bolan lowered his rifle and signaled for him to come out of hiding. "Let's get back to the vehicle. We need to move."

They returned to the SUV and jumped inside.

"They're not risking the chopper," Bolan said. "Right now, they've landed. They're coming toward us on foot. Time we got away from here."

He reached into the rear, where he had put his additional weapons. He grabbed a Glock autopistol and made sure there was a full magazine in place, and that the gun was cocked.

"You ever fire one of these?" he asked Escobedo.

The Mexican shook his head. "Never had the need."

"That day looks like it might have come," Bolan said, handing him the pistol. "Glock 17. It's ready to fire. Just aim at the target and squeeze the trigger. There are seventeen rounds in the magazine. Hit a man and he'll know it. Don't try to be fancy. Aim for the widest part of the body."

Escobedo took the Glock, examining it as if it was some alien artifact.

"I'm not a killer, Cooper. Why would I want to shoot people?"

Bolan revved the engine and spun the SUV away. The AK and Uzi were propped against his seat, his Beretta close in its shoulder rig.

"An easy answer there, Hermano. The men chasing us *are* killers. Unless you want to die out here, you'll have to defend yourself. This isn't the time to get into a debate over moral issues. What it boils down to is whether you want to live and put Seb Jessup behind bars."

Escobedo set the Glock in his lap. "I believe you see life in black-and-white, Cooper. To you there is good and evil. Only dark and light."

"Simpler than I would describe it, but right now that pretty well sums it up. You witnessed something you shouldn't have. Jessup wants to bury you so the story won't come out. Right now we have a group on our backs who want to make that happen. Question is—you happy with that?"

"Of course I don't want Jessup's men to find me. My life may not be as important as some, but it is to me."

"When you witnessed Jessup killing those people, you reacted the way any decent person would.

You wanted to make things right. It meant you put yourself in harm's way, yet you still stood up and offered to help."

"And little good it has done me. Those agents were murdered because they were going to help me. That was when I realized how useless my gesture had been. So I turned around and ran. I came here to hide. Not a very courageous thing to do."

"You were one man. Alone. Unsure who to trust. You acted to protect yourself. No shame in that."

"But it didn't work. Jessup has found me. He sent his killers to make certain I don't return to America and point the finger at him."

"Then we have to make sure he doesn't get what he wants."

"He is a powerful man. He has money. And friends. In Broken Tree he is *muy importante*."

"Broken Tree is a small town, Hermano. Jessup is a big fish in a little pool. If we play our cards right, we can drag him out of it."

A hesitant smile edged Escobedo's lips. "That I *would* like to see."

"If you want to see anything other than the inside of this car again, I suggest you pick up your gun."

Out the corner of his eye, Bolan saw armed figures cresting a nearby ridge. The men scrambled forward, weapons raised. Bolan glanced out the side window. Saw the A La Muerte shooters leveling their guns. Saw the muzzle flashes as they opened fire.

Mariposa's crew had caught up with them, and right now were making their presence felt…

17

Bolan felt the solid thump of slugs against the Escalade. The SUV rocked as he swiveled the wheel. One of the rear windows shattered.

Escobedo was speaking rapidly in Spanish. Bolan couldn't make out whether his words were curses or a swift prayer. The Mexican sat rigidly, his knuckles white as he gripped the Glock.

A figure broke from cover, closer than any of the others, AK raised as he confronted the SUV. Bolan slammed down on the gas pedal and felt the vehicle surge forward. Realizing his foolish move, the A La Muerte soldier made an attempt to pull back. The Cadillac sideswiped him. Bolan felt the impact, caught a glimpse of the guy as he was tossed through the air, arms and legs flailing. He crashed to the ground, his body coming down hard, twisted at an unnatural angle.

"Go left. Go left here," Escobedo said urgently. "This way will take us to the regular trail."

Bolan saw a gap in the thick brush and hauled the SUV around, leaving a thick cloud of dust in his wake. The suspension took the impact of the undulating ground, the heavy vehicle bouncing over iron-hard ruts. The route took them on a downward slope, and after a couple hundred yards opened up onto a defined track.

Escobedo turned to stare out the back window. "This trail will take us to the north."

"They can't follow us on foot," Bolan said. "They thought they could outflank us. It hasn't worked."

"Won't they go back to the helicopter?"

Bolan nodded. That was a given. And once they were back in the air, the chopper could monitor their line of travel from a safer distance. Even call in more ground crews. Any reprieve he and Escobedo had imagined they might have would be short-lived.

"Break out the machine gun," Mariposa said as they reached the helicopter.

Rico already had the rotors spinning, prepared for the crew's return.

"What machine gun?" Candy asked. "Hell, you didn't say you had got a machine gun in here."

"I had other things on my mind," Mariposa said. "Then was not the best time. Now *is* the time." He turned to his crew. "Move. Get it mounted in the door."

Candy watched the cartel soldiers fall over each other in their haste to drag the machine gun from a side compartment, pulling out a metal ammo box, as well.

Why hadn't Mariposa used it before? As an army,

these guys were a mess. Coordination and order were obviously not in their operating manual.

The weapon was an M240, 7.62 mm general purpose machine gun. Candy had used the M240 himself on a number of occasions. He watched the cartel members mount the gun on pintles by the side door. An ammo box was attached and the belt of 7.62 shells placed in the feed tray. The mechanism was closed and the weapon ratcheted to load it.

While they worked, Rico fired up the chopper and it lifted off the ground. He set his course for the fleeing SUV.

"Rico, get us in range," Mariposa said, his voice rising above the clatter of the rotors and the wind coming in through the now open side door.

The chopper turned, angling as Rico hurled it in the direction of the SUV, which was below and just ahead.

Mariposa was yelling at his crew to open fire.

The sudden rattle of automatic fire filled the helicopter as the M240 came to life. Ejected brass casings began to litter the deck. The cartel soldier manning the weapon had his fingers closed tight around the trigger as he sprayed the SUV.

"She's hit," someone said triumphantly. "*Madre*. She is hit."

18

Bolan heard the clatter of autofire and realized the chopper was better armed than he'd thought. There was a machine gun on board. He didn't bother to wonder why it hadn't been used before, just swerved left and right. But the pilot had his target just where he wanted it and the gunner was getting his range and beginning to fix his target.

"Sorry, Hermano. Looks like we may need to abandon ship again."

"Better than waiting until they—"

His words were cut off as a burst of 7.62 mm slugs ripped through the side window behind him. Glass showered across the interior. More bullets pounded the body of the SUV. A tire burst, rubber shredding.

"Now?" Escobedo asked.

"Now."

Bolan hit the brakes and brought the vehicle to a stop, grabbing hold of the AK and slinging the Uzi around his neck. Escobedo pushed open his door and bailed out. The machine gun rounds kicked up dirt around the Escalade as Bolan freed his own door and dived off the seat. He hit the ground in a power roll that took him clear of the vehicle. When he hit, the Uzi slammed against his chest. The AK-74 was almost wrenched from his grasp, but he clutched it tightly.

He heard the roar of the helicopter as it closed in, the continuous chatter of the machine gun. Window glass blew out from the SUV, showering Bolan as he kept rolling. The chopper flew directly overhead, briefly casting its dark shadow across him. He came up on one knee, shouldering the AK, and triggered a long burst at the retreating aircraft, not expecting to score any hits as it sped away from him.

The helicopter made a tight turn and immediately homed in on Bolan's position. It arced to the right, coming at him sideways. He moved just before the machine gun opened up once again, pulling up the AK-74 and returning fire.

Bolan had been hoping for a successful hit. He got more than he expected when the guy manning the machine gun fell back inside the cabin, blood spraying from his chest and shoulder. Bolan kept his finger on the trigger until the magazine was spent. He immediately ejected it and snapped another one into place, then took aim at the helicopter again. His burst raked into the chopper behind the passenger compartment. The last few rounds hammered the tail rotor. Its stability compromised, the chopper wavered in midair. It made a half-circle sweep, the pilot attempting to regain the control that he was losing.

"Smoke!" Escobedo yelled. "Coming from the engine."

Sure enough, oily black smoke was streaming out through several vents. As the chopper lost height, the beat of the engine faltering, Bolan saw it was moving back in their direction—fast.

"Hermano, let's go!" he said.

Bolan snatched the rest of his gear from the SUV, urged Escobedo forward, and they cleared the vehicle and ran.

"THIS BASTARD HAS the luck of the devil," Mariposa said.

"I could call it something else," Candy said.

"Rico, get us down. Now!"

Mariposa's voice could be heard above the unhealthy sound of the distressed engine.

The pilot made a decent job of landing the stricken craft. Despite its ungainly cant during the descent, Rico managed to touch down without breaking the helicopter in half.

There was a wild scramble as the cartel soldiers abandoned their transport, hauling their weapons with them. By the time Candy extracted himself, just behind Mariposa, smoke was starting to fill the cabin.

As they moved away from the downed aircraft, Mariposa started to give out orders. "Find that *yanqui*. I want to cut out his heart and feed it to him."

His crew moved off in the direction of the SUV.

Behind them, the helicopter was belching smoke, the thick clouds darkening the sky.

Mariposa had his sat phone in his hand, making contact with his home base. When he got through he began a tirade in rapid Spanish. Candy didn't even attempt to translate.

"We will have reinforcements coming. It may take a while but they will find us," Mariposa said.

"And in the meantime?"

"We hunt down your Escobedo and his new friend."

Haven't been too successful up to now, Candy said to himself. If Escobedo had stayed on the US side of the border things might have been different. Mariposa and his banditos were making one hell of a fuss, but not scoring many points.

Candy wanted to call Jessup to update him. Problem was, he didn't have a single good thing to say, and he wasn't about to make any criticism about Mariposa and his crew within earshot. So he left his phone zipped up in his pocket. He had switched the thing off, to prevent Jessup making contact from his end.

Candy followed the strung-out line of cartel soldiers trudging across the dry landscape, and tried to put himself in Cooper's position. He and Escobedo were on foot now, having been forced to abandon the bullet-riddled SUV. This was the Mexican's home turf. He would know the way to go, and it was obvious the pair would try for the border. It was still a great distance away. Cooper would have to adapt as he went, but Candy had a feeling that wouldn't be a problem for the man, who seemed to have the ability to improvise around anything that stood in his way.

Makes your damn A La Muerte soldiers look like Boy Scouts, Ramon, Candy thought.

One of the soldiers, ranging ahead of the group, stopped and raised an arm, beckoning for the others to join him. The man was crouching in the dirt when they reached him. He pointed at scuff marks in the dust.

"They were here," Candy heard him say. "They passed a little time ago."

Mariposa examined the tracks, followed their path, nodding to himself. "Still heading north," he said.

He pulled out his sat phone and made contact, reverting again to rapid Spanish. As he spoke, the rest of his crew moved on, following the tracks.

Mariposa nodded to Candy.

"We will have them soon."

THE ONLY THING working in Bolan and Escobedo's favor was the undulating landscape they were crossing. If they had been traveling over an open plain, the pursuing A La Muerte soldiers would have been able to spot them much faster. Still, Escobedo informed Bolan that soon they'd reach flatter terrain.

"We will have little cover then," he said.

In the shade of a small stand of trees, Bolan looked back the way they had come, scanning the slopes they had recently crossed. He had no doubt that the cartel crew was moving along their trail. They were not about to turn around and go home.

He secured his backpack and made sure his weapons were all fully loaded. Escobedo watched him, curiosity in his eyes.

"None of this is new to you, is it?"

"Let's say I've done it before."

"Modest, too," Escobedo commented.

"Is there anything out there?" Bolan asked. "Towns? Villages?"

Escobedo managed a smile. "You mean somewhere we might rent another vehicle?"

"A thought, but I guess not."

"Senor Cooper, we are far from anywhere that could provide such a luxury."

"So no more helicopters?"

"We may be able to hire a couple of burros from a farmer. If we come across anyone who owns them."

Bolan picked up the AK he had leaned against a tree. "Let's go," he said.

They were about to move out when he heard the clatter of automatic fire. Earth spouted into the air only feet away.

Bolan shoved Escobedo aside, saw him stumble, and then spotted a running figure heading in their direction, firing as he came. Bolan dropped to one knee, pulling the AK into position, butt against his shoulder, as he tracked their assailant. He ignored the other man's careless shots, took his moment and eased back on the trigger. His slug hit the target center mass. The guy stumbled, finger still on his own trigger as the muzzle dropped. He blew away half his left foot in a bloody haze, then slammed facedown on the ground.

"Hermano." Bolan stood, turned to where Escobedo was pushing himself to his feet, caught hold of the Mexican's shirt and yanked him upright. "Move. *Move*."

They broke right, keeping the small stand of trees between them and any further pursuers.

Bolan kept Escobedo in front while he monitored the trail behind them. If one of the cartel soldiers had gotten close, the others wouldn't be far off.

"Hermano, do you know this area very well?"

Over his shoulder Escobedo said, "Pretty well. Why?"

"We need cover. Somewhere we can defend ourselves. If they push us into the open they'll pick us off."

"This is very rough country. Not many people. Not much of anything except—"

Escobedo faltered and went down on his knees as the crack of a single shot reached them. He reached up to clutch at the bloody wound in his right shoulder.

Bolan was at his side in seconds, grabbing his shirt again and pulling him back up. "Don't go down," he commanded. "Stop and they'll be on us like a pack of wild dogs."

The Mexican lurched to his feet, lips peeled back in a pained grimace. "I will not give them that pleasure."

Bolan dragged Escobedo behind the closest trees, then turned and faced the oncoming opposition. He saw two of them converging as they approached. Autofire crackled. Wood splintered in all directions as bullets pummeled the trees. Bolan leaned against a solid trunk and raised his AK. He tracked the closest shooter and punched a quick pair of slugs into him, twisting him off his feet and dropping him to the ground. The other man threw a quick glance at his downed compadre. He took his eyes off the ball, and paid for it with a shot through the heart and a follow-up that took his left eye out before slicing through his skull.

Bolan could hear the first guy moaning. He swiveled his rifle around and took aim at the figure sprawled out in the dust. The AK cracked once and the shooter's skull blew apart in a bloody spray.

Bolan turned his attention to Escobedo, helping him to his feet. The bullet had ripped through the fleshy part of his right upper shoulder, missing the bone but leaving messy entry and exit wounds. Blood was oozing from the torn flesh.

"Can you move on?" Bolan asked. "Soon as possible, I'll check you out."

Escobedo nodded. His face gleamed with sweat and he kept his hand pressed to his bleeding shoulder.

"We go through the trees," he said with gritted teeth, pointing at a slightly larger copse a few dozen yards away. "Then there is a barranca a little way on the other side. A ravine. This one is quite big. It runs north for many miles."

It was the best news Bolan could have hoped for. A deep ravine would provide them with some degree of cover, and it would lead them away from the pursuing cartel soldiers. It wouldn't make A La Muerte vanish completely, but it might slow down their pursuit. Anything that might force their enemies to delay their chase was welcome.

Bolan transferred the rifle to his left hand, encircled Escobedo's body with his powerful right arm and helped support the man as they moved through the timber.

Pursuit seemed to have waned for the moment. Bolan knew it would start again once the cartel counted their losses. He and Escobedo needed to use whatever time they had as efficiently as possible. If they managed to reach the ravine, they'd have a chance of getting clear.

They made it through the trees after a five-minute walk, emerging on open ground. Escobedo, despite the pain from his wound, thrust out his uninjured arm, fingers extended.

"To the right. There."

Bolan gazed in the direction Escobedo indicated and saw where the ground dropped away. They'd have to cross a stretch of flat terrain before reaching the ravine. They would be totally exposed to any approaching cartel soldiers. Bolan understood the risk, but knew there was no other choice.

"Hermano, you set? We need to get over there, fast."

"*Sí*, I understand. Don't worry about me."

Bolan smiled. "Oh, sure, that's about to happen."

He tightened his grip around the other man's body, then surged forward, away from the trees and across the open terrain. Escobedo gasped as the jolting aggravated his shoulder, but Bolan ignored the cry. He'd do what he could to treat him once they made cover, but if the cartel thugs located them before they headed into the ravine, there would be no use worrying over a shoulder wound.

Escobedo almost lost his footing a couple times, and Bolan had to keep him upright without breaking his relentless stride. Dust trailed in their wake. The soldier concentrated on the lip of the gorge, pushing away thoughts of what might be at their backs.

The drop-off appeared in front of them. Bolan stared across the twenty-foot span, then down the rocky slope that plunged more than thirty feet to a narrow stream. The ravine wall was craggy, dotted with parched vegetation. The descent would be perilous in some spots, and while he didn't doubt he could scale it safely, it would be a long, slow process, and he wasn't sure Escobedo could manage it with only one good arm.

About twenty feet from where they stood, a section of the rock face seemed to have broken off, covering the slope with loose rubble. It was the only chance of a swift way down to the bottom.

"Was I right?" Escobedo asked, breaking into Bolan's thoughts.

"You were," he said. "Escobedo, you trust me?"

"With my life," the man answered, following Bolan's gaze to the debris-strewn slope. "A bullet in the back, *mi amigo*, or a wild ride down into hell? What choice do we have?"

"You said it. Just hang on."

Then they stepped over the edge.

19

The moment their feet touched the slope, the loose stones and dirt shifted beneath them. Yet despite the uneven surface, Bolan and Escobedo negotiated the rock wall without injury. They slid and stumbled their way down, hitting the ravine floor amid clouds of acrid dust, with pebbles raining down around them. Once they'd come to a stop, Escobedo's strength seemed to fail him; he sank to his knees, blood still oozing from his shoulder wound.

Bolan helped him stand up. "We keep moving north," he said.

"If I had stayed at my place," Escobedo panted, "I would be dead by now. If it wasn't for that fact, I might be angry at what you are putting me through. I hope it will be worth it."

"Stay angry," Bolan said. "Anger is what you need to keep going right now."

They turned north, following the thin stream at the bottom of the ravine, Bolan setting the pace. He wanted—needed—to get ahead of their pursuers. As determined as he was, Escobedo was not going to be able to maintain his pace until Bolan did some in-the-field first aid on his shoulder wound. They had to put as much distance as possible between them and the cartel before Escobedo's strength failed completely and they had to stop. And so far, A La Muerte seemed to be making a habit of catching up.

"EVERY TIME I turn around we seem to have lost someone," Candy said. "It's a goddamn turkey shoot. And guess who's the turkey."

"But he can make mistakes," Mariposa said. "Just like the one he made now. He has gone down into the barranca. He is boxed in. All we have to do is pluck him out."

Candy wasn't entirely convinced. Something was telling him Cooper had chosen the ravine deliberately. The guy was smart enough to understand the risks of going down there. Cooper would have his reasons. This was *not* a mistake. If Mariposa believed it was, he could be setting himself up for a big surprise.

When they reached the spot where Bolan and Escobedo had descended into the ravine, Mariposa ordered his men to go down first, while he and Candy brought up the rear. They slid and stumbled to the bottom, dust swirling around them.

"They will be moving north," Mariposa said.

He issued orders and his crew moved out, searching for signs left behind by the two men they were following.

Candy studied their surroundings. He saw the logic in Cooper's move. The ravine offered cover and he would be able to monitor the position of his pursuers. The man would also realize that coming down here hemmed him in, though that was still safer than staying out on open ground. The rocks and foliage down here, along with the ravine walls themselves, would provide some protection. They would enable Cooper to watch his back as he and Escobedo kept moving.

Cooper had manipulated this situation to his advantage as much as possible, but there was one thing he couldn't control. Candy had seen Escobedo stumble when a slug had hit him. That would slow them down and give the American more to worry about.

Still, Candy wasn't too certain that Mariposa taking his crew down into the ravine was such a wise move. The confining nature of the place left them open to their enemy's AK-74, and he was proving to be a damn good shot. He might even choose to make a stand, picking off Mariposa's dwindling army one by one. Candy hoped the drug boss's reinforcements arrived sooner rather than later.

Much sooner.

ESCOBEDO WAS FADING FAST. He was making an effort to stay upright and maintain a decent pace, but his wound was still bleeding and the blood loss was weakening him. Gripping his pistol in his right hand, his left hand still pressed to his shoulder, he moved on unsteady feet.

The guy was determined to keep going, Bolan saw. But sheer guts wouldn't be enough to keep him standing for much longer.

Bolan was scanning the route ahead. The floor of the ravine was littered with tumbled rocks and coarse scrub. The hard-packed ground was crisscrossed with shadows where the sun couldn't reach. If nothing else, the high walls would protect them from anyone trying for a swift shot. Coming down here wasn't the perfect solution, but it was the best they were going to be offered.

Escobedo uttered a low moan, came to a stop and dropped to his knees. Bolan stood over him, then dropped to a crouch.

"I can't go on anymore… Need to rest…"

Bolan gripped him under his uninjured arm and gently pulled him to his feet. He led him to the side of the ravine, settling him with his back against the wall. Bolan offered him water from his canteen, and while he drank, leaned his rifle against the rocks and took off his backpack.

Finally, the soldier eased Escobedo's hand away from the wound. He saw the hole in his shirt where the bullet had come out. A small advantage; at least the slug wasn't still in there. Bolan peeled Escobedo's shirt back, revealing the puckered hole and torn skin. Blood still oozed from the wound, but it had started to congeal. Bolan opened his pack and removed the small first aid kit.

"Hermano, I want you to keep watch while I deal with this," he said. "You see any of them, say something."

The Mexican nodded. His face was damp with sweat.

Bolan slipped on thin latex gloves, then used a couple antiseptic wipes to clean around the entry and exit wounds. He folded gauze into pads and staunched the holes, back and front. Finally, he wound a bandage around Escobedo's shoulder, looping it under his armpit and securing it with adhesive tape. It was basic, crude medical aid, but it was the best Bolan could offer in the circumstances. He pulled Escobedo's shirt back into place.

"Cooper," his patient whispered. "Thirty feet back. Near the left wall. I see one man."

Bolan reached out slowly and retrieved the AK-74, sliding it into position. He looked back the way they had come, and sure enough, he spotted a man crouched behind a fallen boulder that was about eight feet across. Bolan could make out the guy's right arm and shoulder, and half his head.

And the comset in his exposed hand. The cartel soldier was already speaking into it, checking in with his teammates behind him.

Bolan brought the rifle to his shoulder and sighted along the barrel. He made a quick calculation, then squeezed the trigger, the weapon nudging back against him. The 5.45 caliber bullet caught the man in the head. There was a flash of red from the rear of his skull and he went down and lay still.

Bolan couldn't say how much time he had just bought, but he knew he and Escobedo were short on it. He snatched up his gear and gestured with the rifle. "Let's move."

Escobedo pushed himself to his feet, swaying slightly for a few seconds. "I'll make it," he said. "I won't let them win."

THE ADVANCE SCOUT was sprawled out in front of them. His final message had brought the others to this spot at a run, but by the time they'd reached him, he was down, the back of his head blown out.

Now Mariposa was on his phone, engaged in an aggressive conversation with his home base. Candy had no idea what was happening. Mariposa's wild ranting was lost on him. Even so, he could feel the hostility in the *jefe*'s tone.

What had started for Mariposa as an agreement to help out a friend had transformed into a personal vendetta. The cartel boss had committed men and time to the cause, and the more the American did to defy him, the more Mariposa's need to hunt him down and kill him grew. Cooper was cutting a swathe through the opposition. His skills at evasion and his uncompromising responses were tearing Mariposa's troops apart.

The drug lord had backed himself into a corner and the only way left open to him was to score a victory over Cooper. He couldn't walk away now even if he wanted to.

Pride was one thing, Candy would admit, but Mariposa was taking it too far.

The cartel leader shut off his phone, composed himself, then gestured at the group before him. "I have ordered a crew to make for the far end of the barranca," he said. "If they can reach there before those *cabrónes*…" He gave a characteristic shrug.

Candy fell in with the others and they continued along the rock-strewn path. Altogether, there were five of them: Mariposa, Rico, the two remaining A La Muerte soldiers…and himself.

Should be enough to deal with one American.

Going on numbers alone, it was a reasonable assumption.

But given what had already happened, Candy had doubts.

He hunched his shoulders against the solid beat of the sun and wondered just how he had let himself get drawn into this deal. He smiled at the thought. He knew damn well what had enticed him. The money he'd been offered. Too much to turn down. As always, it came down to the cash. Candy never could walk away from a deal where big money was the sweetener. His weakness. The drug that sucked him in every time.

He couldn't resist the promise of money in his hands. Thick rolls of bills. That always did it for Candy.

And now he was stuck out here in the back end of Chihuahua, tagging along with A La Muerte. Sweating his ass off and tracking two shadows: the guy hauling Candy's target along, cutting down his pursuers like someone swatting flies off an apple pie. And Hermano Escobedo.

The catalyst who had set this whole mess in motion.

If the gardener hadn't stumbled on Seb Jessup in one of his murderous rages and gained evidence that would send the man away, Escobedo would not be on the run. Mariposa wouldn't be involved.

And Candy wouldn't be out in the Mexican badlands, traipsing around like a damned idiot watching the A La Muerte troops dwindle.

The whole affair had come about because Escobedo had been in the wrong place at the wrong time. And of all the men who could have stumbled into a situation like that, it had to be him, a man determined to stand up for "justice."

The son of a bitch had to have been one of those people who couldn't stay the hell away. They saw something they figured was wrong, and felt the need to do something about it. Instead of turning his back, Escobedo had gone yelling to the cops, laying Seb Jessup open to a jail sentence.

What the hell was that all about?

Hadn't the dumb-ass realized he was simply volunteering for the death sentence to come crashing down on his own head? He'd been too eager to play the concerned citizen to understand it didn't work that way. You didn't go around pointing the finger at someone like Seb Jessup, and not expect to have that finger bitten off and rammed down your throat.

Jessup valued his life, but more, he valued his business. Giving it up wasn't in his universe. He had built it from nothing. To the point where it was worth millions. Jessup loved the money and the power. His was a world of take, take, take, and the hell with everyone else. From his hardscrabble beginnings Seb had built his criminal empire by sheer dedication. No one lone Mexican was going to take that away from him.

Ramon Mariposa was driven by similar emotions. Cooper had defied him. Killed his men. Mariposa's pride would refuse to accept those losses. Like Jessup, the Mexican had too much invested to allow a single man to challenge him.

Candy couldn't keep a thin smile off his lips. He was caught in the middle of it all. If Cooper had stayed on his side of the border, back in Texas, Candy could have tracked him and taken the guy out without even setting foot in this godforsaken country. On home ground, he would have had his own boys around him and they would have pinned Cooper down without all this macho bullshit. But Candy was here now, with no way to back out. He gripped his Kalashnikov. All he needed was a chance for a good clean shot and Cooper would be out of their hair. Son of a bitch was good, but a well-placed slug would be better.

20

Bolan and Escobedo pushed forward, aware at every turn that they were still being pursued. The enemy was not giving up.

Bolan's attention was divided between watching the trail behind them and keeping Escobedo on his feet. The Mexican was struggling. Blood loss, pain and exhaustion were threatening to put him down. Yet there he was, still moving, fighting for every step. His face was taut with concentration. Sweat streamed down his cheeks, ran into his eyes. The bandage over his wound was damp with fresh blood.

Bolan heard the growl of a powerful motor somewhere above them. Mariposa had obviously pulled in additional support. It meant there were more A La Muerte soldiers in the area. It also meant transport. Something to consider. With Escobedo becoming progressively weaker, traveling on foot was no longer a long-term, viable option.

They paused in a cluster of man-sized rocks that

would provide cover. Bolan stowed his weapons and gear behind one of the boulders, keeping just the sheathed Tanto knife. He could feel Escobedo watching him closely.

"What are you doing?"

"Trying to get us out of here," Bolan said.

He swapped magazines in the AK and set the selector to single shot, then handed the weapon to Escobedo.

"Stay undercover. There's a full magazine in there. Gives you thirty shots. All you need to do is keep pulling the trigger."

"Saying it like that makes it sound so easy."

"We're running out of options, Hermano. If we keep heading north, they can track us easily. Truth is, you won't make many more miles on foot. We can't turn back, so the only way is up."

Escobedo scanned the rocky slope. "What will you find up there?"

Bolan had no definitive answer so didn't say anything.

"Then be careful," Escobedo said.

"If I was careful I'd be working in an office."

Bolan chose his spot and started to climb. He made his moves carefully, testing each grip and foothold before he added his full weight.

He knew he might be exposing himself to hostile fire when he reached the open ground. Right now he had few alternatives. If he could get to the top and deal with whoever waited there, he and Escobedo might have a better chance of escaping with their lives.

The climb took a little longer than Bolan had expected. A couple times he came across areas where sections of wall had broken off, leaving a smooth, crumbly surface that threatened to collapse beneath his weight. When he hit those spots he was forced to ease to one side and search out firmer terrain.

He heard occasional gunfire as Escobedo squeezed off rounds in the ravine below. He was warning the A La Muerte soldiers not to make any sudden moves, that someone had them in their sights. The standoff was not going to last forever. Eventually some enterprising cartel member was going to go ahead and attempt to earn brownie points by working his way closer. If that happened, Escobedo would have to up the cost by taking a killing shot. Bolan didn't doubt he would do his best.

Bolan kept going, edging his way up the gorge. His muscles strained and his body was slick with sweat. When he looked up he could see the rim of the rock wall and above it the blue, cloud-streaked sky.

He picked up voices above and to his right. Two of them, speaking in Spanish. He strained to make out the conversation, but wasn't close enough yet.

He heard more shots from Escobedo. Some return fire.

Keep them busy, Hermano, Bolan thought.

He hit a stretch of solid rock, dug his toes into the footholds and raised himself a few more feet. The rim was close now. He caught a glimpse of the upper curve of a vehicle roof. The voices were louder. Still off to his right.

"Why don't they rush him? Get it over with."

"Easy for you to say, Lupe. Maybe they don't want to walk into a bullet. We can't see him from up here.

So maybe they can't, either. Who wants to take that kind of risk?"

Bolan flattened himself against the rock. Peered over the lip of the ravine.

A large black Mercedes SUV was ten feet to his right.

Two Mexicans stood by, rifles slung across their shoulders and autopistols on their hips.

Bolan slid the knife from its sheath. He gauged his position, bracing his feet against the slope. His left hand crept over the edge and found a solid grip.

"*Madre*, those chickens down there will die of old age if they don't get something done."

"Don't let the *jefe* hear you call him chicken."

A burst of laughter followed.

That was the distraction Bolan needed. He bunched his muscles and pushed, clearing the rim. He let himself fall forward, tucking and rolling, coming to his feet fast and lunging forward.

The A La Muerte soldiers reacted as quickly as they could, but their responses were seconds behind and Bolan was on them before their coordination kicked in.

He swept up with his right hand and slashed the keen edge of the knife across the exposed throat of the closest guy, cutting him deeply. The Mexican stumbled away, clutching his ruptured skin, vainly trying to stop the surge of blood.

Bolan ignored him as he closed in on the second man.

The guy had offered a swifter response, snatching his AK-74 from his shoulder in the brief moment when Bolan was handling the first man. He swung the rifle like a club and knocked the knife from Bolan's fingers. The Executioner simply kept moving forward, twisting his upper body and ramming his right shoulder into the man's middle. Bolan put all his strength behind the strike and the impact slammed his opponent backward. He hit the side of the truck, breath exploding from his lips. Bolan allowed him no respite. He whipped his right forearm around in a powerful blow that crunched against the guy's cheek. Something snapped. The Mexican's head jerked to one side. Bolan kept up the momentum, delivering a hard kick to his right knee. The force was enough to shatter bone, and the guy slumped forward as his leg gave way. Bolan rushed forward, snaking an arm around his neck and kneeing him in the base of the spine. Dazed as he was, the man was aware of his vulnerable position and tried to fight back. Bolan gave him no chance. The desperate cartel member let go of his rifle and threw up his hands to grip Bolan's muscled arm. Bolan hauled back, putting pressure on his neck. The man struggled, but his exertions only accelerated his demise. Bolan felt his resistance weaken, then cease, the guy becoming a heavy weight in his arms. Bolan lowered him to the ground and picked up the gun the man had dropped.

The Executioner turned his attention to the big Mercedes 4x4. It could be a means of escape for him and Escobedo, but there were still cartel shooters in the vicinity.

And Escobedo was at the bottom of the ravine.

Bolan needed the man back at his side so they could use the vehicle. But the Mexican was in no state to climb out of the gorge solo.

The crack of Escobedo's AK came again. Moments later, Bolan heard return shots. He needed something to hold the enemy back while he got Escobedo out of the ravine.

Bolan retrieved his Tanto and sheathed it. He opened the tailgate. The space behind the rear seat held additional ordnance—backup autoweapons, assault rifles, handguns, ammunition.

A soft canvas tote yielded half a dozen fragmentation grenades. Bolan snatched up the bag and walked along the rim until he was well clear of Escobedo's position. He studied the floor of the ravine and picked up some movement.

A La Muerte.

He heard answering shots to Escobedo's fire.

Bolan took out a grenade and held the lever down as he pulled the pin. Then he launched it, watched its downward curve. Heard the sound as it detonated and saw the brief explosive flash. He followed with a second grenade.

He had already returned to the 4x4 when the second grenade exploded. Even if it failed to inflict casualties, the explosions—and the implied threat of more to come—would hold back the advance for a short time.

Bolan checked out the Mercedes. At the rear was a built-in cable winch powered by the vehicle's battery. He activated the unit and freed the cable, pulling out the thin steel coils. He threw the line over the edge of the ravine, allowing it to snake down to Escobedo's position.

"Hermano! Use the cable," he yelled, and Escobedo's voice floated up from the ravine in acknowledgment. "Loop it round yourself and fasten the eyebolt. Leave the AK."

When Escobedo signaled that he was ready, Bolan went to the 4x4 and set the winch working, slowly retracting the cable.

He kept a lookout as the device hauled Escobedo up the side of the ravine. The two men Bolan had taken out up here would not have been alone. He could expect other cartel soldiers to appear at any moment, and he was ready to face them when they did. He stayed close to the side of the vehicle, watching for any movement that might indicate company.

The cable scraped across the rocky rim, and now Bolan could hear Escobedo's labored breathing as he neared the top. As soon as his head and shoulders appeared, Bolan reached out to stop the winch, waiting until Escobedo was on level ground before cutting the power.

The Mexican struggled to his knees. He had Bolan's equipment and weapons over his good shoulder, and the Executioner moved quickly to take them, then helped him to his feet.

"Not something I would like to do again," Escobedo said.

Bolan loosened the cable, then let the winch retract fully.

"Get in," he said, gesturing toward the 4x4.

The man didn't hesitate. He made his way around the vehicle, leaning against it for support. Bolan had already seen the fresh bloodstain from his wound showing through his shirt.

Bolan opened the rear door and dropped his gear onto the seat.

As he turned to reach for the driver's door, he heard a distant shout, and when he spun around, saw a pair of armed figures moving toward them along the lip of the ravine.

Luck was taking a vacation.

The two were close enough for Bolan to see their raised weapons. He eased his way to the rear of the Mercedes and brought the AK-74 into play, tracking in on the moving figures. One was gesturing with his free hand to his partner as they negotiated the uneven ground.

Bolan hit them with short bursts. His first shots caught one of them in the chest. The guy ran on for a few yards before dropping facedown on the ground. The second man fired at Bolan. Slugs chewed at the rear door of the 4x4. Bolan sank into a crouch, lowering the AK's muzzle, and shot the Mexican's legs out from under him. He saw the bullets tear open bloody wounds. The guy screamed hoarsely, tumbling to the ground. His weapon flew from his hands.

Bolan made for the driver's door, slid inside and thrust the AK into Escobedo's hands. When he fired up the engine the Mercedes burst into life. He stepped on the gas and the vehicle lurched forward, rolling across the rough ground and bouncing both of them on their seats.

"Hey!" Escobedo said loudly, as a figure appeared ahead of them.

Bolan slammed his foot down on the pedal and the heavy vehicle surged forward. The man's expression changed from determination to fear as he realized his vulnerable position. He had no time to react to the change in circumstance. The Mercedes's wide grille hit him full on, lifting him off his feet. The man was thrown across the hood and up against the windshield, where he hung for a few seconds before rolling to one side and vanishing from sight. A smear of blood remained on the glass.

"*Madre*," Escobedo said. "These people do not give up."

Bolan spun the wheel around. "And neither do I."

21

The sporadic gunshots held Mariposa's team back. No one else had been hit, but the drug lord had already paid a heavy price in his pursuit of Matt Cooper and Hermano Escobedo. Though he hadn't expressed his feelings vocally, Candy had the impression the cartel boss was becoming disillusioned.

The survivors of the group were waiting for a backup team to contact them. When the call finally came, Mariposa expressed his feelings in language that even Candy didn't need translated.

"The crew has split up," Mariposa said in English for Candy's benefit. "They are moving along the rim in each direction. Two have stayed by the vehicle."

Candy glanced upward. The afternoon was coming to an end and the light was no longer reaching parts of the ravine, so it would be harder to spot Cooper and Escobedo from above.

"They can't see us. We can't see them," Candy

said. "This is what they call the *enfrentamiento mexicano*."

Mexican standoff.

"You watch too many Western movies," Mariposa said.

Moments later, the first grenade detonated. It had landed some twelve feet from their position. The burst rattled back and forth across the ravine. Debris showered the area.

The pilot, Rico, was closest to the explosion. He crouched, took a run back toward the others and was caught when the second grenade went off. His scream was lost in the burst as he was spun off his feet, coming down hard, his body twisting awkwardly as he landed. His left side and lower back were shredded, shrapnel tearing into his flesh and leaving it raw and bloodied, bone gleaming in the open wounds. Rico convulsed for a few moments before he became still.

"Jesus," Candy said, "this is becoming a fucking war zone."

"Keeping Jessup out of jail is becoming very expensive," Mariposa said. "I hope it will be worth all this trouble."

The A La Muerte boss, one of his soldiers and Candy. They were the only ones left in the ravine.

"How many up top?" Candy asked.

"Five," Mariposa said. He glanced at Rico's body. Faint wisps of smoke hovered over the scorched clothing. "And now I will have to find another good pilot."

"Not the most moving eulogy I ever heard," Candy said under his breath. "I'm sure the guy's mother would be comforted at that benediction."

"*Jefe*, what do we do now?" the cartel soldier said.

Mariposa managed a smile. "A good question, Alvarez."

"You think Cooper will be open to a bribe?" Candy asked lightly.

"No," Mariposa said, "I believe he just wants to kill us."

From above came the sound of gunfire. Then silence, followed by the rumble of an engine starting. The noise faded as the vehicle moved away.

Candy said, "I think we've been abandoned, old buddy. Something tells me Elvis just left the building."

Trembling with controlled rage, Mariposa took out his sat phone and began to issue orders.

"This is not over," he said when he ended the call. "Those two still have to get across the border."

Candy took out his own phone and made contact. When Jessup came on the line Candy brought him up to date with the situation.

"Am I hearing this right?" the Texan asked. "This Cooper yahoo has run rings around Mariposa and his army?"

"Seb, he may be a yahoo, but he's a smart one. We don't know jack shit about his background, but the guy knows combat. He works tactics. And he doesn't take prisoners."

"Well, give the man a round of applause. I don't care if he has a Congressional Medal of Honor. I just want him dead, alongside that sneaky Mexican asshole."

"Ramon is callin' in some more backup," Candy related. "Soon as we have them we'll move out."

"Looks like *I'd* better have some boys ready at this end. You know, just in case they slip by you hotshots."

The sarcasm wasn't lost on Candy. Jessup cut the call without another word, leaving him staring at the dead phone.

Maybe I should hang on to that down payment, Candy thought. Sounds like Jessup might want it back.

He glanced down at Rico's bloody corpse. Could be the pilot took the easy way out. Whatever lay ahead of them, Candy wasn't exactly looking forward to it.

He caught a glimpse of Mariposa. The cartel boss had a tense expression on his face. His eyes darted restlessly back and forth as he stared at the confining walls of the ravine. He was letting the situation get to him. This was not what was supposed to happen. The drug lord was used to being in control, dictating the action and making others pay for challenging it. The American, Cooper, had changed that. He had snatched away the man they were after, and had inflicted telling casualties on A La Muerte.

Candy knew that Ramon Mariposa was committed now. He had no choice. The American had to die, alongside Escobedo. Nothing less would satisfy him. Nothing less would restore his challenged authority.

22

The day dimmed around them. Shadows lengthened. The landscape lost its definition as the night pushed in. Bolan drove steadily, negotiating the terrain with care. Beside him, Escobedo was fast asleep. In his weakened state he needed his rest, and Bolan made no demands on him. The man had already gone through enough.

When darkness cloaked the land, Bolan rolled the vehicle to a stop. Driving with headlights in this empty landscape would be like painting a bull's-eye on themselves, but continuing on with nothing to light their way would invite other risks. They couldn't afford to lose another vehicle.

Bolan sensed Escobedo stirring. He glanced over, to find the Mexican working something out of a side pocket of his pants. He offered a small, wrapped object to Bolan.

"If anything happens to me, Cooper, this will back up my evidence."

Bolan took the package. "Hermano?"

"It is the SIM card from my phone. It has the video of Jessup murdering those young Mexicans. The murders I witnessed."

"Nothing is going to happen to you, Hermano. I'm going to see you get to safety."

"*Sí*, I understand that. But just in case things don't go as we plan, this will explain everything. Promise me you will see it gets to the right place."

Bolan slipped the package into one of his blacksuit's zippered pockets.

"You *both* go with me," he said. "And you both get to be delivered."

Escobedo laughed. "You sound like the US Mail."

Bolan held the Uzi close as he leaned back in his seat. "Right now, we could use the express delivery service."

He took out his sat phone and contacted Stony Man. Barbara Price's smooth tone filled his ear when she picked up.

"Hey, Striker, been a while."

"It's been a busy time down here."

"This a sit rep?"

"I have our guy sitting next to me."

"But?"

"But we could have non-friendly locals on our six. Can you get an eye on us?"

"I'm on it. I'll come back ASAP."

Bolan felt Escobedo watching him.

"Was that help you were calling for?"

"Could be"

"I hope it was. Cooper, after everything that's happened, tell me it is all going to be worth it."

"We'll get to see Jessup locked up. The A La Muerte cartel will be minus one head piece of trash and down a number of soldiers. What's not worth it about that?"

"Whatever you say," Escobedo said. "I am too tired to argue."

His words trailed off. He was too weak to stay awake, so Bolan let him sleep.

23

First light. Shadows retreated as the day dawned. Bolan drove the Mercedes in a half circle so he could scan the surrounding terrain. The satellite imagery Price had pulled up was now proving correct. Two vehicles were moving to intercept him. They were coming fast, leaving thick dust streams in their wake, converging on his position with the intensity of ravenous sharks. They were coming in for the kill.

Braking hard, Bolan shook Escobedo awake, barking at him to crouch in the foot well and stay down.

Escobedo's eyes shot open and he slid silently into cover.

Bolan picked up the AK-74 and switched the selector to full-auto. He reached for the canvas bag holding the remaining grenades, then pushed open the door and slipped clear, crouching near the Mercedes's front wheel.

The closest of the approaching vehicles was already turning to confront him. The other held back, allowing the lead 4x4 to make the play. Bolan gauged distance. They were already within range of his rifle. The lead vehicle slowed, the windows opening as gun muzzles were pushed out. One AK-74 spat a tongue of flame and Bolan heard the bullet strike the hood of the Mercedes. The shot was followed by more, the offensive fire taking out the windshield.

Bolan came up enough so he could lean on the side wing to steady his aim. He focused on the oncoming 4x4 and depressed the trigger. The AK-74 hammered out its full clip, pouring thirty 5.45 caliber slugs at the oncoming vehicle. The windshield blew in, showering the occupants in glass. Bolan saw shadowy figures inside jerking under the unrelenting stream of bullets. The 4x4 came to a shuddering halt, engine stalling, for the driver had been hit. By this time Bolan had dropped the empty magazine and slotted in a replacement. He raked the 4x4 again.

One rear door opened and a bloodied figure tumbled free and dropped to his knees. Bolan sighted in and hit him with a short burst that put him down for good. Then he spotted someone exiting on the far side of the vehicle. The guy ran to the rear and moved to the corner closest to Bolan, poked his rifle around the vehicle and opened up on him. Slugs peppered the Mercedes. Bolan heard a tire go with a hiss of escaping air. The vehicle sank onto its rim.

Out the corner of his eye, he saw the second vehicle pull back and sit waiting.

The concealed shooter started firing again.

Bolan put down the AK, took out one of the grenades and pulled the pin. He moved behind his vehicle, using its bulk for cover as he launched the grenade at the 4x4. He sent it toward one of the bullet-shattered windows. His aim was good and the device dropped inside.

It blew out the side panels as it went off, the harsh crack of the detonation followed by flame and a cloud of smoke. There was a second blast as the fuel tank exploded. The ravaged vehicle was engulfed in flames. Metal fragments pattered to the scorched earth.

The gunner concealed behind the 4x4 was thrown from his position like a human fireball. When he hit the ground, he thrashed about, slapping ineffectually at the flames consuming him, his shrill screams giving way to rapidly diminishing whimpers.

Bolan pushed himself upright and circled the blazing wreck, the Uzi in his grip now. The thick smoke covered his movements. He heard the growl of the other vehicle as it nosed closer, and heard raised voices as the A La Muerte crew took in the scene of destruction.

Bolan peered through the haze and made out moving figures ahead.

He counted four of them.

"THIS TIME HE does not walk away," Mariposa said.

He followed his two soldiers out of the 4x4.

They fanned out, their forward vision hampered by the fierce flame and smoke from the wrecked vehicle.

"A bonus to the man who brings me the heads of Escobedo and that damned American."

Candy hung back. He could see the way this was going. Cooper was getting them to do exactly what he had planned. Drawing them clear of their own vehicle while he used the cover of the burning wreck.

Candy moved to the rear of the 4x4 and edged around it until he could see Cooper's vehicle. If the American was on foot, Escobedo would be alone inside the Mercedes. Cooper wouldn't want him exposed to hostile gunfire.

Which could make this the moment Candy fulfilled his own contract.

This was his chance.

He heard the crackle of automatic fire as one of Mariposa's guys opened up.

The other men were all engaged. This could be his opportunity.

Candy measured the distance, saw smoke drifting his way. He broke cover and ran toward the Mercedes. Smoke stung his eyes. He could stand that.

He heard more autofire.

Someone yelled, and not in celebration.

THE A LA MUERTE SHOOTER had mistaken drifting smoke for a human shape. He triggered a burst and ran forward to follow it up. He paused when he realized he'd wasted his moment. Only then did he see a more substantial form emerge from the haze.

There was no mistake this time.

Bolan's Uzi crackled, and the bullets tore into the target's body, breaking ribs. The cartel soldier uttered a startled yell. Bolan fired again, this time sending the 9 mm slugs into the guy's skull.

As the man dropped, Bolan cut to the side, still making the most of the smoke. It wasn't going to last as cover, so he needed to stretch his luck.

CANDY SAW MARIPOSA'S man go down. The cartel boss signaled to his remaining soldier to circle around, and moved forward himself. Then a tall figure emerged from the drifting smoke. Cooper.

The man was impressive, his black-clad form imposing. Candy could see why the American had survived everything thrown at him. His movements were controlled and confident. It was plain to see why he had defied the A La Muerte soldiers. This was more than a simple gunman; he carried himself with the ease of a man totally in harmony with himself. A formidable enemy. He was a soldier in the true sense of the word. A fighting man who had no need to broadcast his skills. The evidence was in his actions.

Slipping past Cooper and the fallen cartel guy, Candy reached the rear of the Mercedes. He looked in through the passenger window. There was no sign of Escobedo. The vehicle seemed empty.

Where was he?

The Mexican couldn't have left the car. If he had, he would have been spotted. There was nowhere to hide.

Candy inched along the side of the Mercedes, still not satisfied.

He peered into the rear window, seeing nothing, then yanked open the door…and met the muzzle of a Glock. Hermano Escobedo was pointing the pistol at him, and thrust the barrel forward as he lunged up from the floor of the SUV.

Escobedo looked like a man on his final stretch. He was disheveled, with dark rings around his eyes, his face beaded with sweat. His clothes were grubby, and bloodstained around his right shoulder. He braced himself with his left hand, but the hand holding the pistol was surprisingly firm, with no sign of a tremor.

"You see what you have done to me?" Escobedo said quietly. "What you have made me do…"

ESCOBEDO PULLED THE trigger and put a 9 mm slug into the man's face. It hit him between the eyes and cored into his skull. The man's head snapped back with the impact, so the second shot Escobedo fired struck lower, smashing in through his nose. His opponent made no sound as he fell to the ground, his AK spilling from his hands.

Escobedo watched him fall, his own finger squeezing the Glock's trigger a few more times before it locked empty. Tears streamed down his face. He leaned against the edge of the seat, drained and exhausted. At that moment he had no resistance left in him.

BOLAN MOVED INTO the clear, the smoke behind him, and saw the surviving pair of A La Muerte soldiers facing him. They were both carrying AK-74s. He counted off the seconds as they both swung their rifles in his direction. Bolan took the only offensive action he could. His hand went into the bag slung from his shoulder and he brought out one of the remaining grenades. He dropped his AK and pulled the pin. The instant he threw the grenade, he grasped the Uzi.

The grenade hit the ground and bounced, catching the attention of Mariposa and his man. It detonated with a hard sound, throwing up a shower of earth and a deadly spray of shrapnel.

Mariposa went down as fragments ripped into his

lower legs. The A La Muerte soldier survived the blast because he was slightly behind Mariposa and was shielded. He caught fragments of shrapnel in his right arm, but not enough to take him out of the fight.

Bolan turned the muzzle of his Uzi on him as the last man standing twisted away from the grenade burst. Bolan triggered the SMG, his shots finding their target. The cartel soldier doubled over as he took a gutful of 9 mm Parabellums. Bolan stood, moving to end his agony with a short burst, then turned to stand over Mariposa.

The Mexican drug dealer stared up at him, his face screwed up from the pain of his shredded legs. Bloody shards of bone showed in the ravaged flesh.

"You know who I am?" Mariposa asked, hands pawing at the ugly leg wounds.

"No one important," Bolan said.

"I am Ramon Mariposa. *Jefe* of A La Muerte."

"If that's supposed to impress me," Bolan said, "it doesn't."

"I know who you are," Mariposa said. "Matt Cooper. When Jessup finds you and that cockroach Escobedo, both of you will die…"

The Uzi moved. Just enough.

"You first," Bolan said, and pulled the trigger.

The drug dealer's face vanished in a mess of flesh and bone.

BOLAN FOUND ESCOBEDO passed out in the Mercedes, the dead Texan on the ground by the vehicle. Escobedo held the empty Glock in his hand.

"Good for you, Hermano," Bolan said.

He crossed to the SUV the Mexicans had been using, and climbed in behind the wheel.

This is becoming a habit, he thought.

He drove up alongside the Mercedes and transferred Escobedo into the backseat. Then he gathered his gear and placed that on the floor beneath the passenger's seat.

According to the satellite data Stony Man had sent, the border was a couple hours' drive away. Bolan used his sat phone GPS to plot the route, and pulled away from the smoldering, bloody scene of the firefight.

An hour later, he called Stony Man and spoke to Hal Brognola.

"I'm roughly an hour from the border. Hal, I need to be met by a medical team. Escobedo has a bullet wound in his shoulder. He's lost blood and right now he's unconscious."

"Okay, Striker. Barb will have a fix on your position. We'll have a team waiting. I need to ask this. Is there a trail of bodies littering the Mexican landscape?"

"Only bad guys, Hal. Members of the A La Muerte cartel. Including, apparently, the head honcho. Ramon Mariposa has been permanently retired."

Brognola sighed. "Sounds like I have a few phone calls to make."

"Mexicans are not going to miss Mariposa and his crew. Except maybe a few who were on his payroll."

"That is a sad indictment of our society, Striker."

"You think."

"But true."

Bolan failed to hold back a smile. He could understand the Big Fed's view, but as far as he was con-

cerned, having Escobedo in the rear of the SUV made
up for what had gone down. Hal Brognola was prone
to seeing things from the dark side. Part of his job
was handling the flak when matters got out of hand.
Brognola managed it with consummate ease. He had
become adept at defusing political gray areas.

Bolan, for one, would always be grateful for the
Big Fed's skill at smoothing over troubled waters;
often waters Bolan had stirred up. The Executioner
had no time for niceties or appeasement. The people he faced on mission after mission were long past
words. They let their weapons speak for them. Bolan
was pushed into the position of dealing with the fallout of violent actions.

Brognola said, "Still, this is going to take some
sorting out. Okay, let me make those calls. We'll send
someone to meet you at the border."

"Hal, things didn't go too well last time. Escobedo
has to be placed in secure hands. Nobody local. Bring
in people from a distance."

"You think Jessup might have paid help?"

"Somebody picked me up when I crossed the
checkpoint. They must have. That was the only way
Jessup could have known I was on my way into Mexico. They had my vehicle details. Mariposa had a crew
on my tail almost from the start. You guys have to
bring in people with no connection to Seb Jessup."

"Can you stay out of sight for a while? Give us the
time to pull in some help?"

"Not too long, Hal. Hermano needs medical aid
as soon as we get to the border."

"If I have anything to do with it he'll have the best.
Call you back."

24

"So where are you talking from now?" Price asked.

"Hotel in Texas," Bolan said.

"All over then?"

"You could say that."

"Why are you being so mysterious? This a national security issue?"

Bolan chuckled softly. "Miss Price, your suspicious side is showing."

"Striker, what's going on? I understand things were hectic down there."

"Still are," Bolan said. "It got a little hot when we hit the border. Only just managed to stay ahead of the Mexican police. That's being worked out even as we speak."

"Seriously?"

"The Mexican authorities are calming down now that they see the damage done to the cartel. Especially the removal of one Ramon Mariposa. After Brognola contacted the Texas Rangers and explained the situation, they agreed to act as intermediaries in getting me and Escobedo out. They sent a unit down to the border in a Texas Department of Public Safety helicopter. Had a Ranger squad on board, plus a couple of medics. They crossed the line and took us up just before the local Mexican cops arrived."

"How did the police know where to find you?"

"From what we worked out, the Mexicans received an anonymous tip about us. It came from either the cartel or Jessup's organization. Making a last attempt to silence Escobedo."

"Sounds close."

"That kind of close I can do without," Bolan said. "In any case, the Rangers took us to Austin. Way out of Jessup's bailiwick. He might have influence, but not with them."

"Men in Western boots and big Stetsons," Price said. "Now, how is Escobedo?"

"In hospital under Texas Ranger protection. He's recovering. Despite what he went through, he's coming through okay. He swears he'll attend the trial even if he has to crawl on hands and knees to be there. I believe him."

"And Jessup?"

"The main attraction? In a cell," Bolan said. "With his legal team screaming blue murder."

"Will he get away with what he did?"

"The video Escobedo took identifies him without argument. It's not pleasant viewing, but Jessup can't wriggle his way out."

"People have got away with worse," Price noted.

"The evidence is pretty damning. Hal told me that after the Feds saw Escobedo's video, they had their people go over the barn. And guess what? They found blood traces. Human blood. That gave them grounds to search the whole property. Turned up the baseball bat. Blood on it matched the traces found on the barn floor. Along with Jessup, there were at least three of his men on the video."

"No trace of the bodies?" Price asked.

"Not yet."

She was quiet for a moment. "Has this happened before?"

"FBI labs found other blood traces on the baseball bat. Apparently, they're processing them as we speak. And other teams have descended on Jessup's property, going through everything they can lay their hands on. Since Escobedo's story came out, a couple other workers at the estate have come forward. They've given statements about suspicious things that went on around the place. Looks like our friend Escobedo has started the beginning of the end for Jessup and his business."

"If Jessup walks after all this I'll shoot him myself," Price said.

"No," Bolan said quietly, "that will be my job."

He knew Price would understand he was not making light of the threat.

He was, after all, Mack Bolan.

The Executioner.

* * * * *

COMING SOON FROM

GOLD EAGLE ®

Available June 2, 2015

THE EXECUTIONER #439
BLOOD RITES – *Don Pendleton*
When rival gangs terrorize Miami, Mack Bolan is called in to clean up the city, but the mess in Florida is just the beginning. The drug trafficking business is flourishing in Jamaica…along with the practice of voodoo and human sacrifice.

STONY MAN® #137
CITADEL OF FEAR – *Don Pendleton*
Able Team discovers that Liberty City, an economic free zone in Grenada, is a haven for building homemade missiles. Phoenix Force arrives just in time to provide backup, but the missiles have already been shipped to a rogue group with their sights set on the California coast…

SUPERBOLAN® #174
DESERT FALCONS – *Don Pendleton*
In the Kingdom of Saudi Arabia, a secret group is plotting to oust the royal family. Their next move: kidnapping the prince from a desert warfare training session outside Las Vegas. Mack Bolan must keep the prince safe—but someone in the heir's inner circle is a traitor.

COMING SOON FROM

GOLD EAGLE ®

Available July 7, 2015

THE EXECUTIONER® #440
KILLPATH – *Don Pendleton*

After a DEA agent is tortured and killed by a powerful Colombian cartel, Bolan teams up with a former cocaine queen in Cali to obliterate the entire operation.

SUPERBOLAN® #175
NINJA ASSAULT – *Don Pendleton*

Ninjas attack an American casino, and Bolan follows the gangsters behind the crime back to Japan—where he intends to take them out on their home turf.

DEATHLANDS® #123
IRON RAGE – *James Axler*

Ryan and the companions are caught in a battle for survival against crocs, snakes and makeshift ironclads on the great Sippi river.

ROGUE ANGEL™ #55
BENEATH STILL WATERS – *Alex Archer*

Annja uncovers Nazi secrets—and treasure—in the wreckage of a submerged German bomber shot down at the end of WWII.

"Please, get me out of here!" she begged him. "I can pay you!"

"That way," Bolan said, nodding toward the hallway leading to the back door, "while I cover you."

She ran, and Bolan retreated from the staircase, walking backward as he followed her, still covering the Viper Posse shooters on the second floor. Each time one showed his head, Bolan squeezed off a round or two and sent them ducking out of sight.

He heard the back door open as the lady shoved against it, bursting out into the night. She might run off without him, and if so, he wished her well. The last thing Bolan needed was a sidekick looking for sanctuary.

But she didn't run. He found her waiting in the alley, looking frantic. "Don't tell me you *walked*," she implored.

"The car's down that way," Bolan told her, pointing. "Half a block."

"You'll take me out of here?"

"I didn't plan to hang around."

"Please hurry, then, before they catch us!"

She was off and running after that, with no idea what Bolan's ride might look like. To delay pursuit, he fired another short burst through the open door, no targets yet in sight, then followed her at double time.

"The Mercury," he told her as he caught up.

"This? It's old."

"It's vintage," he corrected, and unlocked the doors remotely, sliding in behind the wheel while she sat next to him.

Downrange, he saw armed men erupting from the back door of their social club, scanning the alley and the street beyond for targets. Bolan left his headlights off as he revved the Marauder's engine, cranking through a tight U-turn, even though they were sure to spot him anyway. Less than a minute later, he had two cars in pursuit and gave up the deception, switching on his lights.

"We can't outrun them in this…this…"

"Don't underestimate 390 cubic inches," Bolan said, still not entirely sure he wanted to escape from Channer's men. More damage could be done by getting rid of them for good, but he required an open killing ground for that, without civilians in his line of fire.

"They're coming!"

"Stay down after we stop," he told her.

"Stop! What do—"

"Hang on! We're almost there."

Don't miss
BLOOD RITES
by Don Pendleton,
available June 2015 wherever
Gold Eagle® books and ebooks are sold.

GEXEXP439

Bolan charged down the hall, greeting every challenge
with a snarl of bullets, blasting craters into the torsos of
El Tiburon's fighters. Some of them wore body armor, but
the M4's deadly sputter struck with enough force to slow
them down, allowing Bolan to adjust aim and put bullets
into their exposed heads and throats.

The Executioner surged across the ground floor, his
senses fine-tuned to everything around him. Between
Rojas's sniping, Bolan's blitz and the gunmen's agitated
state, Los Soldados de Cali Nuevos didn't stand a chance
in this tenement.

It took all of a minute and two 30-round magazines
to completely clear the first story. The second story was
alive with breaking glass and screams of terror and pain.
Rojas wasn't allowing the Soldados a moment of respite.

Bolan had supplied the woman with low-light and
magnification optics which could squeeze every ounce
of accuracy out of the rifle, and from the sounds of it, she
was taking advantage of her concealed position.

She'd obviously done a lot of long-range shooting,
even though the distance wasn't great. At most, her
shots would have to travel forty yards, but even so, her
accuracy and the sheer amount of destruction she was

wreaking on the tenement were impressive. By the time Bolan reached the second-floor corridor, only a few men remained within sight. They were cowering in a corner, seeking protection against the drywall.

The Executioner shouldered his rifle and drilled one of the men through the side of his head with a single round. The other Soldado let out a scream as he saw his friend's head go to pieces, and waved his machine pistol wildly. In the dark hallway, Bolan was a wraith among the shadows.

Bolan ripped the terrified gunman open with a tri-burst from his compact rifle, eliminating that threat before continuing across the floor.

"On two," Bolan told Rojas. "Don't shoot me."

"Wouldn't dream of it," La Brujah replied. "I'm saving all my ammo and hatred for the enemy."

Don't miss
KILLPATH
by Don Pendleton,
available July 2015 wherever
Gold Eagle® books and ebooks are sold.